D1784134

Endorsements and Reviews

Our past can keep us imprisoned. Dealing with our emotional past is important to move forward in life. In *The Beckoning Rooms*, Karin takes her reader on a journey from hurt to healing.

—Kary Oberbrunner, CEO of Igniting
Souls Publishing Agency
Author of *Unhackable, Day Job to
Dream Job* and *Elixir Project*

• • •

Understanding the origin of our pain is the start of our personal evolution into achieving happiness. In order to find this light, we need to look no further than ourselves. We are our best friends in this journey. *The Beckoning Rooms* help us explore this through fictional characters, who are beckoned to search deep within themselves as they go through the rooms.

—Andrea Musso, M.A.

• • •

"To die, to sleep—to sleep—perchance to dream..." Famous words indeed. But let us leave the question of dying for another occasion and let us focus on the issue of dreaming.

Everybody dreams, no question about that. But what do we do with our dreams? Some people remember them a little bit but don´t do anything with them. Some people remember them and are able to talk about them, with espouse, family and friends, or perhaps with their analyst. Others simply forget them. Others, like S. Freud, write them down, reflect upon them, and try to understand them. In fact, thanks to the genius of Freud and his work *The Interpretation of Dreams*, we now have a better way to understand the nature of dreams.

According to him, the origins of our dreams can be found in events that occurred during the day, or in events occurring in our own Unconscious. Usually, these have to do with basic impulses that are unacceptable to us, due to our own upbringing, our values, our beliefs and so on. Because of this, we tend to *repress* our dreams, and that is why we forget them. In fact, according to his view, the content of dreams constitutes the basis of anxiety, which is the direct result of the *sinister* (Das Umheimliche), which refers to that which is supposed to remain permanently hidden, suddenly seeking to manifest itself to Consciousness. In fact, in this sense, the *sinister*, that which is frightful, that which is dreadful, usually relates to many things familiar to us since childhood but that have been repressed. This "known but unknown" biographical material ("There is a lot we don´t know that we know," says Jenna in chapter ___), returns in our dreams and is then experienced as something strange, as something *sinister*.

This is why, from the beginning, Jenna says to herself: "Maybe I'm not supposed to remember…maybe I am just supposed to figure it out. But with what purpose?" With what purpose indeed! And that is precisely what makes this book worth reading. It will invite us, through the dreams of Jenna, Jeremiah, and Jacob, to face a number of strange situations which will force them to ask themselves very pertinent questions regarding their own inner truth, questions which, I am sure, the reader has also asked himself at some point in life. These are *The Beckoning Rooms*, which, as author Karin Brauner suggests, we either deal with them, or they will deal with us.

Very entertaining reading, with a very important message throughout, which has to do with the quest of self-discovery: "True knowledge comes from within," she says; "Look inward for knowledge...own your truth...trust your truth... explore it and act accordingly".

And that makes the book worth reading!

—Luis A. Recinos (Guatemala, January 12, 2021)

• • •

Excellent! Sort life out, or it will sort you out.

The Beckoning Rooms is a fast-moving work of fiction that had me gripped from the outset. More to the point, the moral of the book is crucial: that problems, even if unpleasant, need to be dealt with rather than hidden from. One way to do this is to examine one's past: what formative experiences have led you to this point? Are you depressed, addicted, lacking in confidence, etc.? What has caused you to feel this way, and—above all—how do you fix it and move on? How do you become the best version of yourself?

Meet Jenna, Jeremiah, and Jacob, three characters with traumatic pasts who find themselves thrust into an unexpected but very necessary situation. They must now confront their demons in order for life as they know it to resume. I found each of the protagonists to be relatable and unique in voice, especially Jacob (owing to my own experiences of therapy). However, Jeremiah's story also made me emotional.

All in all, [this book is] definitely a page-turner, and one that—in spite of being the author's first attempt at fiction— sits finely among my other collection about a troubled adult's relationship to their tortured ego.

—Andy Beck, musician, multilinguist, and author of *Folk Springs Eternal*

• • •

Reading *The Beckoning Rooms* was quite an experience. Karin Brauner Hollman skillfully draws you into a world where you're unsure whether the characters are actually living through their experiences or are in a dream world.

I found myself identifying with the characters to differing degrees and learning new things about myself in the process.

I could sense the influence of the author's counselling background, but she doesn't bash you on the head with it; its in keeping with the flow of the story. A fascinating book that will speak to ever who reads it.

Highly recommended.

—Tayo Igbintade, BSL/English Interpreter, Parent
Advocate, Author of *Adventures at the Seaside:
A Children's Book About Sibling Relationships,
Empathy, Tolerance and Acceptance of Difference*

THE BECKONING ROOMS

DEAL WITH THEM OR THEY'LL DEAL WITH YOU

Thanks for being a part of
the book launch!

I hope you's enjoy this
book and your e-book
version of 20 Self-Care
Habits

KARIN BRAUNER

Karin Brauner
08/07/2021

Published by Author Academy Elite
PO Box 43, Powell, OH 43065
www.AuthorAcademyElite.com

Identifiers:
LCCN: **2021903701**
ISBN: 978-1-64746-734-0 (paperback)
ISBN: 978-1-64746-735-7 (hardback)
ISBN: 978-1-64746-736-4 (ebook)

Available in paperback, hardback, e-book, and audiobook

Other books by the author

20 Self-Care Habits (first edition)
20 Self-Care Habits (2021 Edition)

"This above all, to thine own self be true,
And it must follow as the night the day,
Thou canst not then be false to any man."

—Shakespeare, *Hamlet*

TABLE OF CONTENTS

Jenna

Jeremiah

Jacob

A New Life

JENNA

CHAPTER 1

Unfamiliar Surroundings

Jenna woke up feeling refreshed. She hadn't slept like that in a long time. As her eyes adjusted to the darkened room, using the sliver of light coming in through the blinds to her advantage, she rubbed her eyes and tried to focus her sight. The blackout blinds blocked most of the sunlight. Stretching, Jenna thought, *I have to go to the shop today, or I will have nothing to eat, and more importantly, no toilet paper—now that could be a catastrophe!* Attempting to get her still-drowsy self up and ready for the day, she started to get up on the left side of the bed, as usual, but her momentum came to an unexpected stop. "Ouch!" Paralysed by the pain inflicted by the unexpected thump, Jenna managed to refrain from shouting expletives while she rubbed her head.

What is that doing there?! Jenna reached out her hand and felt a cold, solid structure before her, which stretched as wide as she could reach. *What? A wall? That's not meant to be there! The wall is on the other side. I better turn on a light, but if my bed isn't in the right place . . . where will the light switch be?*

Jenna cautiously rose from the bed. With one hand in continual contact with the wall-like fixture, she noticed the cold that was radiating from the wall to her hand as she slid it across while searching for the lightswitch. It took a moment for her eyes to adjust when the bright light flooded the room, but she immediately realised she wasn't in the room she went to sleep in the night before. She narrowed her eyes as she looked around, brows furrowed in confusion. Despite not knowing where she was, she felt amazed at how familiar the room looked.

She knew all of the items that were there—some of them she hadn't seen in years. *Teddy! Oh, how I used to love making imaginary tea for you! My old skates, now that brings back memories.*

A bit puzzled by it all, Jenna paused to ground herself. She was confused, but she was experiencing so many feelings and had so many questions. *Why am I here? How did I get here? Am I still asleep right now?* These thoughts bubbled in the back of her mind. Somehow, though, she wasn't scared at the idea of not knowing where in the world she was.

The familiarity of the long-lost treasures she was reacquainting herself with helped, for sure. But how was this even possible?

There has to be some explanation for this!

Jenna looked out the window, hoping to see her lovely landscaped garden that backed to the neighbour's garden, but she was surprised by what she saw: a vast field, nothing else in sight.

How did this happen? I haven't been drinking, and I wouldn't end up in a completely different part of the country or anywhere but my own home anyway if I had been drinking. I came home and went to bed in my own bed, in my own house . . .

Where is this place? And how did I get here?

Jenna realised as soon as her stomach made an empty grumbling sound that she was going to have to leave that room and find food. *Leaving this room would be an interesting concept, indeed.* She checked herself again and gave her forearm a pinch. *Nope, still not drunk, and ouch! I felt that.* Standing in the middle of the room, Jenna looked around and discovered more and more items she'd sent to the memory bin of her somewhat-uncomfortable past. Touching the objects brought back memories of the good times she'd had with them. A slight smile formed as a tear simultaneously fell down her cheek. *Well, nothing has happened yet, except that bump on my head from hitting the wall.* She reflexively rubbed her forehead again; it still hurt.

The door beckoned to Jenna. She tiptoed over and rested her ear against the wood. Silence.

Hmm, it might *be ok to go out there. I don't know whose house this is, but then again, it's the only place for miles, by the looks of it. I can always replace the food I eat. Whoever—or whatever—put me here had to know I'd get hungry and need the essentials.*

Jenna shook her head and chuckled silently. *Wait a minute, replacing used items is what I'm thinking about? I should be worrying more about how I got here and why I'm here! Maybe there's a letter somewhere for me. Maybe I need to figure this out on my own. Oh my, what did I get myself into this time? Wait a minute. I know I didn't get myself into anything. I went to bed—in my bed—and woke up here. Wherever here is.*

The door propped Jenna up while she spent another few minutes pondering her predicament, considering her options. There didn't seem to be any from her standing point in that strange-but-familiar room.

I could stay here until night-time, go back to sleep, and hope I wake up in my own bed in the city.

Time will pass very slowly if I do that, she thought, *and what if there's no way out of here, and I wake up here again tomorrow morning?*

The only immediate choice was to open the door and hope for the best.

When Jenna opened the door, she felt an immediate sense of *déjà vu.* But that phrase didn't quite describe what she was feeling. It wasn't simply a feeling of having lived this already. She felt a sense of remembering, like a "tip of the tongue" kind of thing, but with a whole experience rather than not being able to make a word materialise. She had really been there before.

Jenna wracked her brain, thinking about whose house this might be and when she might have visited. Why did this house seem to be somewhere she spent a lot of time in the past?

I wish I could find my phone! But would it work in this place? I could ask my mum or dad where I was. But would they be able to tell me? Have I been here with them? Did I have a holiday with friends here? It just doesn't make sense. Why can't I remember?

Jenna's mind was racing, trying to make sense of her strange situation. *Maybe I'm not supposed to remember; maybe I'm just supposed to figure it out. But with what purpose? What is going on? What am I meant to figure out?*

She paced behind the still-closed door, practically fuming. *This is all nonsense, figuring things out, calling my parents, remembering . . .* Jenna paused with a sigh and turned the doorknob. *Maybe I'll feel better once I've eaten something.*

The dimly lit hallway had little side tables on either side, coated with thick layers of dust. It was obvious that things were missing, as there were less dusty parts of the tables. While Jenna thought it was odd, she kept walking, not able to come up with a reasonable explanation. *Nothing's sensible about this place so far.*

The hallway was also lined with closed doors. Curiosity got the best of Jenna, and she grabbed one of the door handles. Suddenly, she had an overwhelming feeling in her gut—a warning—that told her to be cautious, as she didn't know what might be behind that door. Did she really want to find out yet—or ever?

As she stood there, contemplating the caution feeling, her body suddenly felt weak and frail. She pressed her hand against the wall for support; it felt cold on her hand, just like the wall she'd banged her head on earlier.

What did that mean? Was she supposed to open or not open doors in this place? There was too much to think about and so many questions creeping over her.

She remembered the same feeling in grade school when she was made to feel she shouldn't question what her parents and teachers told her. She felt that whatever she said was either wrong, not quite right, or laughable. The message was: don't ask any questions; just follow the rules.

Wow! Where did that come from?

Jenna realised the feeling that she couldn't ask questions made her feel as small as she was back in grade school. It was a debilitating feeling which frustrated the heck out of her. But of course, she had been told not to challenge the adults in her life by any means.

Awful! How dare they dictate over my life like that?

Jenna felt exactly that—dictated over like she was unable to decide for herself what was right, what was wrong, or what rules she could choose to follow. She wasn't even clear as a child about what the rules were, and she certainly had no clue what the rules were at this house with its closed doors and no other people to ask or talk to.

How very bizarre.

She wondered if there was any tea—that might help calm her down and give her time to think about what she'd woken up to. But where was the kitchen? Jenna remembered having the last teabag the previous night at home, and there wasn't much milk left either. *Ah well, if this isn't my house, maybe it's at least well-stocked.* She stared at the door a moment longer before leaving to find the kitchen.

Inside the kitchen, she found everything she needed, including food for lunch and dinner—no need for her to go to the shop for now. She paused with a sudden realization. *Would I even know where the shop was? There were only fields all around me.*

As she poured water into the kettle and found the teabag, milk, and sugar for her drink, Jenna felt as if in a dream state. She recalled having dreams about unicorns and fantastic lands back in grade school. *Dreaming and daydreaming about fantastic lands really helped me survive that time.* She let her tea brew for a few minutes, patiently waiting for the right colour, well aware of the situation she was in, but at the same time trying to ignore it for a little bit. *Just for a little bit.*

The tea was nice. Jenna pushed away from the table, ready to find the answers to some of her questions. *I need to find something out about this place and why I woke up here.*

As she walked back to the bedroom, the only familiar room so far, apart from the kitchen, she passed the front door. Jenna checked and it. *No way I'm getting out of here with that door locked and no key in sight.* As she continued down the hallway with those mysterious closed doors, she had another memory. This time the feeling was more like when she was going to university for the first time. She had left the comforts of her familiar school—with all her friends and classrooms.

Walking towards the front door of the school, she remembered walking with trepidation, slowly counting her steps as a distraction to what she would find inside.

It was a scary prospect to be the new kid, to meet new people and make new friends.

But why do I need to make new friends? I like the ones I've had all my life. Oh, right, they're moving away soon to university. Maybe I can see them after my last class. But some might not finish until later or finish even earlier and are already busy with their new friends. Will they forget me? Will they want to meet with me to catch up? This is horrible and exciting all at once.

Jenna remembered feeling guilty about wanting to meet new people and make new friends. She felt guilty about expanding her horizons, about learning new things about life and in her classes, without the usual bunch of people she'd been doing that with all her life.

A feeling of shame for feeling so scared was also forever present during this time. Jenna could almost hear her parents and teachers—those same ones who told her to follow the rules and look pretty: "*It's time for you to grow up, go to college, and choose what you're going to do with the rest of your life. Go on, just get on with it, will you?*"

It seemed like this time she had to tell herself to *go on, just get on with it*, and it made her cringe. Resentment arose even at the feeling of having to force herself to open those doors, with finding out why she was there, and what she was going to do with the rest of her time there.

Was she annoyed at herself for feeling this way or at the adults in her past who made her think that was the only choice back then? Now, she was thinking as they did—she couldn't help it and felt powerless even at that moment when nobody was telling her that anymore. Jenna was overtaken by the voices of her past. *Get on with it; you have to get on with it. Everyone does it. Why are you so worried? Just follow the rules!*

More thoughts flooded her already confused mind— thoughts she'd buried deep down years ago. She didn't want to think about these things. *Ugh, too much. Stop that. La la la la. Don't go there. I'll deal with that later.*

As she arrived back in the bedroom, Jenna shook the feeling off; she didn't like them. She focused on the beckoning doors instead.

CHAPTER 2

Under Fire

As Jenna sat on the bed, she tried her best to calm down, to gather herself from the overwhelming feelings she was having—overwhelming yet familiar—she decided to get up and started to look around the room. Every step she took, everything she grabbed, gave her a jerky sensation in the depths of her mind.

Something unexplainable was happening. Words weren't enough to describe the experience. *Dark but safe is the only way I can describe what's happening right now. Why is this happening, though? To me, of all people?*

She held different items she recognised from her past, spending some time with each of them, touching them, smelling them, remembering. Some smelled like new as if they'd just been brought from the shop. Others had that feel of wear and tear. She spent a lot of time with some of these things and only brief moments with others. She felt oddly grateful for that moment.

Even so, other memories flooded her mind.

• • •

My stuffed animals! I remember you guys. Mum had hung up a hammock-style thing on my bedroom ceiling, where we kept you all. Jenna picked up a pink bunny. She wiggled its ears and lifted it into the air like she'd done so many times while she still had him. She sat down with it as she reminisced over times long gone. Times where she lost herself in her own world. *I loved sitting and imagining we were in magical lands, where we would play for hours on end, not a worry in the world.*

I'd make you tea, feed you grass and dirt in the garden—Mum didn't like that; she said it would make you messy, and you wouldn't be allowed back in. I didn't mind the dirt or the grass; you were mine, my friends! As she remembered this, she brushed some imaginary dirt off of the pink bunny. This brought a smile to her face, but also some resentment was brewing beneath.

One day, I came back from school to find you all gone. It really upset me. I cried but was told it was ok to let go of things and just move on with my life.

You were just stuffed animals to her, but to me, you were my friends. Oh, the fun I had playing with you guys. I so missed you!

• • •

Jenna kept exploring what else she could find in the bedroom. She encountered lots of toys and other things taken from her without asking or without considering how important they were to her. *Not like it was the first time that happened; it seems to be a theme in my life.*

Oh, look! My colouring books! Wait, could it be possible? Yes, it is. My giant colour-by-numbers book. Hello, my old friend.

As she flipped through the pages, Jenna recalled some good times—she'd sit near the window, at the spot that got the most sunlight and used all her crayons, markers, and pastels to make masterpieces out of each picture.

She loved picking the best colours for each part—some were absolutely outrageous: a cat with purple hair, multicoloured clouds, bright red tears . . .

Boy, did I have some imagination! What was I thinking colouring tears red? I must've been going through something, But hey, aren't we all going through something at one point or another?

She loved every single page of that book. Her favourite was her multicoloured unicorn, with some smaller creatures climbing up trees and hiding in the nearby bushes, all happy to be there.

The best ones were hanging on her wall until she turned fourteen and was told to "grow up." *Stop thinking about that; it's in the past. There's nothing we can do about it now, is there?*

● ● ●

Jenna wasn't ready for the next thing she found under the bed. It was dusty and showed signs of age and abandonment.

My music box!

She opened it, and, to her amusement, it still played. The quiet, soothing music coming out of it reminded her of those still moments—many moments—she spent in her bedroom, crying, thinking, trying to understand things as they were happening.

She shrugged the bad stuff away and held on to the nice feelings she had when listening to that lovely tune. Jenna took a few moments to sway back and forth, dancing around the room, holding on tightly to her beloved music box as she did—temporary bliss.

Jenna left the box open, humming the tune as she explored her belongings. As she did so, she noticed a change in the tune. It shifted. It wasn't as peaceful and soothing any longer.

She stopped in her tracks and turned around. Even the little doll standing there was moving quicker, changing her dance to match the new tune that was emerging.

Unreal! Is the freaky stuff ever going to stop in this place? Something inside of Jenna moved, and she thought. *Oh, we're only getting started? Getting started with what? I bet it has something to do with those rooms.* Jenna knew she had to look into those other rooms, despite the tightening in her chest when she thought about it. It felt like the temperature in the room increased, and she started to sway, feeling like she might vomit.

Hesitating. Jenna considered her options. She bargained with herself and the big empty house but realised she wasn't going to get out easily. How she knew that, she wasn't sure. She scrunched her face as she wondered how this was even possible and opted to leave it for now. No answers were forthcoming.

Jenna picked up the box, and as she moved around the house, the tune kept changing. It slowed down as she made her way towards the kitchen, then sped up as she approached those spooky doors that were closed but calling her towards them. Beckoning.

The box seemed to be a good radar of what was going on for her in this place, so she decided to carry it with her while she was in that "magical" house.

After a short while of wandering, Jenna found herself back in front of the first door—the one that'd given her the emotional jolt earlier.

She placed the music box on the floor of the hallway, opposite the first room. The door was still closed shut. Echoes of her previous feelings as she considered going in the room tingled throughout her body, and she told herself, *Go slowly.*

Jenna sat down next to the music box and leant on the wall opposite the dreaded door. Remembering words from her past . . . a poem she'd written . . . Daydreaming . . .

I Am Happy When I'm Me

Playing, Reading, Sleeping
I am happy when I'm doing these.
Fighting, Shouting, Weeping
I just want to be at peace.
It doesn't have to be hard
It just has to make sense to me.
Don't give me any kind of award
Just let me be me.

As Jenna came back to the present, wondering why that old poem she'd written was coming back to her as if she'd barely written it a few seconds ago. She hesitated a bit longer, collecting herself—and her nerves—getting ready to open that door. When she sat in the hallway, the music from the box became noticeable again. The tune sounded a bit confused—just like she felt when she wrote that poem. *Also, a bit like how I'm feeling right now, to be fair.*

I must've been around twelve or thirteen. Talk about a confusing time. I wish I'd known then what I know now, but such is life, huh? I just "had to get on with it." I remember enjoying being in my own company, losing myself in my books that took me to wonderful places.

Remembering some of those fantastic, beautiful places helped Jenna find some calm, as she continued to bargain with herself and the door in front of her, calling her to come in. Her heart was racing as her shaking hand clasped onto the music box. She took herself back to her fantasy world: there were fairies, unicorns, unknown beings walking on fluffy clouds. These were her favourites when she was younger. Later on, she moved on to darker stories, mainly Stephen King. He was her favourite. She learned a lot from him—more than she did in sex ed. *Gee, that guy is imaginative. I wish I could write like that. I guess I should be grateful for all my poems I've written.*

Jenna read to distract herself from things that were going on in her life. Her parents did their best, but she was left feeling lonely and inadequate. She questioned herself, everything she said, and everything she did.

All of it was grist for the mill of judgement; everyone had an opinion:

"Why are you reading again? Go get some friends."

"You play too much. At some point in your life, you have to get serious and choose what you want to be."

"You'll have time to sleep and rest when you're old."

"Being difficult isn't going to get you anywhere. Listen to me or else!"

"What's the point in crying? It won't solve anything."

She went back to thinking about the magical lands and distant worlds she visited and the people and beings she met on her journeys. From mystery to thrillers, from poems to short stories to novels—she just couldn't get enough.

Just remembering those stories helped Jenna forget about the task at hand. Even staring at the door she was meant to go through meant nothing. She was far away, safe from anyone and anything, lost in her memories. Another poem from her teens came to mind. As with the books she chose to read, her poems became gloomier as well.

Darkness

Time is fleeting,
Time changes things.
I can feel my heart beating,
Oh, what I would do with a pair of wings!

How did I get to this dark place,
When did I arrive?
What do I have to face?
To live, to survive.

Within me, there's fear,
Anguish and anger combined.
I can't allow anyone near,
They can't know what's on my mind.

Darkness follows me along.
This new friend is as good as any.
My Journey is long.
I will always have my own company.

I remember being seventeen when I wrote that. Darkness, huh? Talk about putting it lightly. I don't know how I managed to make it, after all that happened that year. Wait. If I remember all these things out here, I wonder what will happen when I go into that room? And there are three rooms to explore.

She didn't enjoy that time of her life. It all seemed to go wrong for her, in more ways than one. All the voices that kept telling her that her ways were wrong. All the glares and stares. Her mother was very particular indeed. *I'm glad I don't live there anymore. I love my home, where I can truly be me, without severe judgement and chastisement at every move I made. No respect.* It shook her to the core, but she was a trooper and kept going like she'd learned to do from a very young age.

Independent and strong—she had no choice. Jenna was her own best friend for a long time. She had some friends and even a few close friends she could trust. But this was something she'd had to deal with on her own. From the outside, it looked like a happy family, but once you closed the door, you could see that it wasn't so. It was subtle, but it impacted her in more ways than one.

This last thought brought her out of her thoughts and back into the reality in front of her. *Ok, that's it. I better get up and go into this room. Let's find out what the heck is going on with this house and with me waking up in it.*

As she got up, the music box again changed its tune. This time, the melody was quicker, faster-paced, as if it knew something about what Jenna would find on the other side of that door.

It took her a while to get the courage to take a step towards the door. Her heart felt like it was going to beat out of her chest. Her mind was all over the place, and she couldn't slow either down.

As images of what could happen went through her mind like flashes of light, she took a deep breath, and took two steps toward the door, grabbed the door handle, and opened the door with her eyes focused on the dancing doll atop the music box.

As Jenna walked into the room, the music box went berserk. She never knew the doll could move so fast. It looked like it could break at any moment, but it didn't. *Ok, little doll in the music box—my new radar or thermometer of what's about to happen next. What are you trying to tell me?*

Jenna finally looked up from the music box. What she saw left her stunned.

It was the first bedroom she ever had. She lived there for a long time. Her heart fluttered at the memories she had in that room, and a soft smile pulled up the tense corners of her mouth. The stuffed animals, the colouring books, the books of poetry, short stories, and novels she'd read there. She loved that room. It was her safe haven from everything else going on around her crazy house. *Amazing.* She thought as she looked around.

Her favourite bedsheets were on the bed. Of course, they were the ones with the unicorns and fantastic creatures print that was starting to fade and tear from being washed and used so much. But she still loved them. *I loved how soft they were from all the times they had to be washed and put on my bed again. I wasn't able to sleep with anything else. It's a wonder these weren't taken away from me. Small battles won, I guess.*

As Jenna sat on her old bed, she felt an immense sense of shame coming over her. It seemed like a long, long, long time since she'd felt that way. She grabbed onto one of her stuffed animals on her bed, clutching it tightly to her stomach, and rocked back and forth in the same way she did when she was younger. The feeling of helplessness swept over her. She was young, still trying to find her way in the world, with very little guidance. *Mis-guidance*, she thought.

After shedding a few tears while hiding her face in her dusty old koala bear, Jenna gathered some strength from knowing that she wasn't that young anymore and that she'd worked through a lot of this stuff as she grew up and saw the reality of the world outside her home. Other people had different relationships with their families—nice relationships.

Jenna latched on to other friends' parents for guidance and for some sort of reassurance that there was nothing wrong with her like she had been told. They were all very kind to her, and even though they didn't know how Jenna felt inside, they gave her the same kindness they gave their own kids: reassurance, hugs, care, encouragement. These simple things were alien to her, as all she felt she got from her parents was criticism and "stiff upper lip" style comments. She couldn't bear it. As she remembered this, even though it was still so powerful, she felt somewhat detached from it.

Oh! Look at that! My playdoh! She grabbed the tubs and opened them up. Moulding them into familiar figures that she'd made so many times in her past, Jenna felt like things were becoming clearer. She remembered particular incidents from her past that left her feeling ashamed. Unexpectedly, she started to cry and become more and more upset as the memories came up.

"Get out of your room right now. Go walk outside and see if you can find someone willing to play with you, weird child!"

"You better eat all that's on your plate. I don't work hard just so you can throw it all in the bin."

"Are you crying again? What happened this time? It was probably nothing. You always cry over nothing."

"Like anyone is going to want to be your friend with that attitude, young lady!"

"Why did you make me shout at you? Why do you always do this? You always lead me to shout and to get angry! I was feel-

ing fine until I saw you sitting there, with your giant colouring book, wasting your time on mindless activities. You'll have to get on with it soon; you're not getting any younger!"

Jenna recalled an incident when she was playing outside with her dolls, making them a picnic of sorts. She was enjoying having a chat with them. They'd talk about the weather, what they would become when they grew up, what her boyfriend would look like when she was old enough to have one. She'd made up this whole fantasy world that sheltered her from her current reality of undermining, ridiculing, dismissing, and her parents not trying to understand her one single bit.

One afternoon, Jenna's mum and dad walked out into the garden, and without saying a word, they picked up her doll friends, all her picnic set, and put them into a dust bin.

As this was happening, Jenna was crying and asking them why. The only answer she got was, "You're too old to be playing with dolls. You should know better. This is childish, and you know it." But Jenna didn't know it. She was quite content in her own world, with her own made-up, quiet but respectful friends.

That was only one of the incidents that she grew up with. Constantly in fear of her favourite things being taken away from her, Jenna had a hiding place behind the shed, where she'd sneak to when everyone was asleep. Fear of the dark wasn't an issue, as she focused on saving her things from her mean parents.

Jenna turned in a slow circle. All the things she'd hidden behind that shed were staring right back at her. *Oh, the joy!* She giggled like a little girl, picking up each toy, book, and treasured thing she'd cried over so many times—in secret, of course. Crying wasn't allowed, not over silly things anyway. *Harsh!* she thought.

Suddenly, one day they moved to a new house. While the plans were made months prior, Jenna wasn't informed. When it finally happened, they all had left in such a hurry that she didn't have time to go and retrieve the items from her shed. She'd thought she'd lost them forever.

Get over it; you'll find new stuff, she told herself, mimicking what she'd heard all her young life. *Oh yuck,* she thought. *I'd forgotten I'd started speaking to myself like that. I guess when you're convinced by your parents that something is wrong with you and that you're going to need to grow up soon and get over it, get on with it like they had to do, then you start to believe it yourself.*

● ● ●

It seemed like she'd been in the same position, clutching her stuffed animals, for a long time. The bright sunlight coming through the window when she first walked into the room was replaced by the glow of the moon. She walked toward the window and stared at the moon for a while. As she started to lose track of time again, her stomach told her in no unclear ways that she hadn't eaten all day. Somewhat reluctantly, Jenna placed the animals neatly on the bed, picked up the music box, and exited the room.

As she walked toward the kitchen, unkind memories of her past continued replaying in her mind, but she tried to counter them with nicer ones. There were few nice memories, but the ones she could conjure up were helping her work through the very difficult memories she'd uncovered in that room.

Oddly enough, the music box returned to its original, soothing theme. As Jenna took a deep breath, she felt emotionally raw. She'd journeyed back through the wonders of memory time-travel to those painful times she'd so longed to get away from. As a grown woman, she could revisit them with fresh eyes, full of new knowledge and understanding of herself. *It still hurts, though.*

She still struggled with shame, feelings of helplessness, wondering if she was right or wrong in this or that choice or situation she'd gotten herself in—be it choosing universities, her course choice, or the friends she'd made as she grew older and became braver and more able to communicate with others her own age.

The struggle is real, she thought as she walked toward sustenance.

Jenna took a deep breath and told herself she was ok. It was all going to be ok. She lingered in the kitchen while she ate a sandwich with some crisps and fizzy water, and then took herself back to her new bedroom. All of the thinking and emoting left her feeling exhausted. A good night's sleep was called for. Tomorrow would be a new day, with renewed energies and two more rooms to explore.

When Jenna finally settled into bed for the night, her thoughts were still actively searching for meaning. What Jenna experienced throughout her upbringing was all leading her to understand that she'd been under narcissistic attack for the better part of her young life, up to when she moved to University.

She found this out long ago by searching on Google for "why do I keep getting attacked by my parents." This led her down the rabbit hole of narcissism and childhood emotional neglect. Both were well researched, with lots of support groups, where Jenna felt she'd found mirrors of herself. Others were struggling with similar, and sometimes, eerily, they experienced the same things from their parents, teachers, romantic partners, friends, and more.

Jenna remembered how relieved she felt when she found out she wasn't alone, that she wasn't weird or "wrong" like she'd been told all along; that's when she started to heal.

Wow! I'd put that away to the back of my mind for so long, but I'm kind of glad this room is showing me what I went through and how I overcame it. Well, some of it anyway. I imagine that I still need to work on some things. Otherwise, I wouldn't be here.

Is that what this whole experience is about? I'm still not sure, but it sounds like whatever it is I'm doing here is not going to waste.

Jenna was pleased by her realisation. Remembering that day when her toys were binned as she was playing happily with them in her fantasy world, she understood her thought of "it's not going to go to waste" was a counter-argument to what her parents used to tell her all the time: "You're wasting your time; you're wasting our time; you're wasting your life on nonsense."

Jenna felt sleep closing in on her and shut her music box, which took about a minute to stop playing—*weird; it usually stops as soon as I close it.* She finally understood that the music box was mirroring how she was feeling. As she closed her eyes and started to drift off, so the music box also faded away into the background, leaving peace and quiet all around.

CHAPTER 3

It Was Never There to Start With

Arising from her slumber, Jenna couldn't have felt better. *Nothing like a good night's sleep to help process the mess that was unearthed yesterday in "Door 1." Yes, I think I'll call it that. I like it.* She'd felt exhausted after emotionally re-living all the things she thought she'd put behind her.

The room brought up vivid memories and strong emotions, including her prized possessions hidden behind the shed—and hidden away in her unconscious a long time ago. Hidden, probably, to alleviate some of the pain she felt after losing her first home, the toys themselves, and the hope she had for keeping some of the few friends she'd eventually managed to make, as her parents forced her to go outside and meet people her age. Deep in thought, she made it to the kitchen.

Jenna realised she was missing something as she sat with a bowl of cereal—Fruity Pebbles, of course (*very apt since it's been my favourite cereal for the longest time*). She pondered her next predicament while staring at her music box, the doll gently dancing for her to the soothing tune. *But what is it? What am I missing exactly?*

She felt an emptiness, like a darkness taking over—similar to that poem she had read the day before. Was she going into her older teenage years in this next room? *Oh, gosh no,*

I don't want to go there. There was so much pain there. I can't imagine reliving it.

But then again, I did "survive" the last room. Staring into space for a few moments, her whole body felt overwhelmed with the gut feeling that this would be too much. They were hard times for her. Memories flooded her mind in such a quick sequence, she could hardly keep up. It was all a blur, but it was intense nonetheless. Growing up—and even now as everything flashed through her eye's mind—Jenna had a sense of betrayal by those who were meant to love and nurture her. Instead, she was stared at like she was from another planet; everything she did was wrong. *That was hard stuff! What a euphemism that is, but I'll go with that for now.*

What is this emptiness I feel now? What's going on? I'm not even in the room yet!

Jenna finished her cereal—how did the house people know it was her favourite? How was any of this going to make sense in any way? Wait until she told people—if she ever got back home. The situation she found herself in was still surreal, but she felt more at ease with her unusual circumstances—as at ease as she could be, without knowing what the heck was going on and how she'd gotten there.

On her thoughtful walk from the kitchen, the music box started playing a sad tune. It slowed down—the opposite of what it was doing the previous day—before she entered the first room.

Jenna, just as she'd done the day before, sat in front of Door 2, staring at it and contemplating what she'd find.

As she was doing that, another poem she'd written came to mind:

Numb

Words won't be enough
But I'll do my best.
When times are tough,
When everything feels like a test.

I just want to stay still.
To lie in my bed.
To hide so my emotions don't spill.
So I can dream of better days ahead.

I feel numb.
It's just as overwhelming
As feeling everything.

Numb.
Everything hurts,
But nothing hurts,
All at once.

I hope this feeling passes soon,
I can't stay in bed 'til noon,
And then stay up all night, staring at the moon.

I can't go on living life like this,
Numb is not an alive state.
I want to experience joy and peace,
I want to clean the slate.

After Jenna cleared the tears from her eyes, she stood up with her music box and walked towards the door. She wasn't afraid, but she felt unsettled, an eerie feeling sending shivers through her spine. As she noticed the goosebumps covering her arms, the music box began its soft, numb-like tune again, ever so slow, ever so gentle, but a harbinger of things to come.

Jenna took a deep breath and opened the door. She found herself inside her teenage room, a room from another house than the childhood bedroom she visited the day prior. It wasn't Jenna's favourite room or place to be. The town was weird; the house was strange; the people there were odd. Plus, people always told her she was weird.

Weird. Those words—weird, strange, odd—ring so true of so many memories I have of this house and this time in my life. It was like starting over again, but with the same narcissistic abuse. Even so, she knew that being older meant she could defend herself a bit better. Obviously, she couldn't defend herself directly from them—that was something she'd learned early on. Standing up for herself would only make things worse.

So, Jenna defended herself internally. She figured out she had the power to deflect what was thrown at her—not to let the arrows hit her directly. She could stop them—kind of like Neo in *The Matrix*—and look at them right in front of her, then move to the side so they'd pass by without hurting her.

She loved that film. It felt so empowering, and it woke her up to her ability to believe in herself, no matter what others told her. After all, the Oracle told Neo he wasn't the one, as a test.

If I am weird and wrong all the time, I'll take it as a test and prove them wrong once and for all! This thought permeated through Jenna's life since she watched that film and began discovering who she really was.

She was lucky to have found friends who showed her that being herself was ok, and, in fact, necessary. While she sometimes mused about how they were, she knew the answer:

they didn't have her parents. *I'm sure their parents had issues, nobody's perfect, but they seem to have good relationships, most of them anyway.*

It was refreshing to see good, positive parenting, even though it wasn't her reality. She often spent time at her friends' houses and got the same treatment they received—she was listened to; they spoke to her with respect; they complimented Jenna on how pretty she was or how good she was at this or that; and they even shared how much they appreciated her and enjoyed having her visit.

At first, it felt weird to hear those positive comments, and she didn't know how to react to them. But eventually, she learned to give the appreciation back and say how grateful she was that she could spend time at their houses and thank them for their attention.

Her parents didn't understand why she spent so much time away from home. After all, in their previous house, Jenna spent a lot of time alone in her bedroom or doing her "weird" picnics with her stuffed animals. Despite their confusion over their daughter's change in behaviour, they didn't try to stop her—Jenna imagined they were pleased to have her out of their way. As much as that hurt, she was glad to have *them* out of her way and not intercepting her outings like she thought they might. It was sort of a win. Bittersweet but still a win.

As she thought about that, she felt that tug of numbness and emptiness inside. *Well, if yesterday I explored my younger years, and that revolved around the way my parents treated me and the ongoing pain that has brought to me even now—I guess today is a chance to explore my late teens and see what happens.* Jenna felt like she better understood her childhood trauma and finally gave responsibility to her parents for what they did—and what she allowed them to do—to her.

• • •

The room was exceptionally bright because of the huge window in there. It was as if it was luring Jenna toward it. The music box started to play a melancholic but faster-paced tune. As she looked through the window, she saw a younger version of herself and her best friend talking with her parents. Her younger self looked at them fondly, and they reciprocated the gaze. When they spoke to Jenna, they also had kind looks in their eyes, like they were paying close attention and asking questions about what she was telling them.

Remembering that particular day, Jenna thought, *Gosh, that was nice. I loved to go to their house. I felt loved and accepted, just as I was. Nothing I said was silly or stupid, and they never considered me as being weird. I was who I was, and that was fine.*

As she continued to look out the window at the scene, she appreciated how real it seemed. After all, she wasn't watching tv or anything. Everything seemed to be happening right outside—in real-time! Watching the scene unfold, she noted how she was beaming, joy reflected in her eyes. There was also something else. Tears came to her eyes as she recalled what she'd felt all those years ago.

Sadness. A longing to have that relationship with her parents. It was a wish that she'd grown up with these parents instead of her own. Along with this came a sense of guilt for feeling that. After all, she'd never lacked food or clothing, or nice holidays, or things to play with. But that wasn't enough. There was so much missing in her life growing up.

The hurt and pain this brought up made Jenna start sobbing. The music box's tune shifted to a dramatic melody, very apt for the moment. She sat on the floor next to the window and wept for what seemed an eternity. As she cried, she felt better, somehow. She felt cold, which usually happened when she cried, so she found her favourite blanket, distantly curiously about how "they" knew to put it there.

Emotionally exhausted and comfortable under her blanket, sleep quickly came over Jenna. While still in the second room, she drifted off into a vivid dream—something of a wishful one at that.

Jenna: Hi Mum and Dad. I'm back.

Mum: Oh, hi darling. Did you have fun?

Dad: I bet she did. She loves it over there!

Jenna: Yes, I did, actually. We had a picnic in the back garden. We even had a fire going and made some s'mores. I'd never had them before; they were great!

Dad: Oh, that sounds lovely, Sweetie, but what are they?

Mum: You haven't had a s'more? We have to correct that right away! They are cookies with melted marshmallow in the middle. They're quite a treat.

Jenna: Yes, please, I want more of those yummy things. They were delicious!

Mum: Ok, hun. We'll get a little fire going later, and maybe you and I can go to the shop to get your favourite cookies and some marshmallows, and we'll be all set for our own picnic!

Dad: Sounds like a great idea!

Jenna woke up with a jolt. Startled by this dream, she looked around; the light outside had faded, the sun was setting and realised she'd been asleep for a while. She grabbed a few more tissues from the nearby box she'd previously procured for herself—she cried quite a lot as she watched the scene from the window.

After tucking the tissues in her pocket, Jenna got up to have a look outside; the same view she'd had before the "vision" (that's what she decided to call it) was back. She gazed out at a green field, not her best friend's garden. As she recalled what happened and the dream she'd had, she realised what she was wondering about at the start of the day was what she'd seen in that vision.

She was missing that feeling of unity, of understanding and respect, of being heard and paid attention to by her friends' parents. *Don't get me wrong. I'm glad she had the parents she did; I wouldn't wish narcissistic attacks on anyone, let alone a child or teenager. But hey, that's the card I was dealt. I survived it, only just. I was lucky I didn't try to hurt myself, is all I'm going to say.*

Now back to what I was missing . . . It hurts to even think about it and to consider it. It's hard to imagine a different life with my parents. That dream was so real, though. I wish It had been true, but it wasn't; it was just a dream.

Jenna decided she'd done enough crying and mourning for what she didn't have. She decided to console herself and think of people that made up for the childhood emotional neglect she'd suffered. Not everything was terrible. Her family had a couple of good moments, but they were very few and far between, compared to the bad-mouthing, gaslighting, and so on.

Suddenly, the memory of a teacher Jenna had in the new school she went to who took her under her wing came to mind. The kind woman combed her hair when she'd forgotten to before leaving her house. She'd listen to Jenna's made-up stories, which were full of fantasy, wonderful lands, and far away places, where everything was beautiful and perfect. This memory made her smile, and her tears started to subside.

The music box changed tunes again, and this time it was playing a more hopeful melody.

How is that music box doing that? It's like it knows what I'm going through and giving me some background music to fit exactly with how I'm feeling.

Jenna remembered her friend's parents again and how loving they were towards her friend and her. They respected her need to recoil, as they understood, without saying a thing, that she wasn't used to this. Eventually, the recoiling subsided, and Jenna could throw herself into a huge cuddle with them and enjoy the nice feeling it gave them all. She was happy when she was with her friend and her parents. So much so that she almost moved into their house. They would make jokes about it, and she was sure they would've been more than happy to take her in.

There were lots of people in her life growing up who compensated for the things her parents couldn't give her.

What my parents couldn't give me, she thought. *Now, that makes it feel a bit less like they did it on purpose. It's not that they wouldn't; it's that they didn't know how. It doesn't make it right or better for me, but it makes sense—if you don't know how to do something, how can you do it?*

A sense of relief came over Jenna as she explored this new way of thinking about her upbringing. It gave her solace to understand that it wasn't that she was "wrong" in any way. It wasn't that she had done something to bring shame to her parents, and in turn, to herself, as they blamed her for how *they* felt. It also wasn't that they had planned it. They just didn't know how to do the things that came so easily to her friend's parents.

Feeling compassion for her parents was hard; she could feel her body back away with the thoughts she was having. Somewhere deep inside, she knew it was the right thing to do if she was going to be able to move forward with her life. Jenna had sort of achieved it, but these thoughts always came back, full force, especially when she felt lonely or like something wasn't going as planned.

Man, these rooms are something else! First, I get reminded of the narcissism I was exposed to. Now, I have to deal with the sorrow of not having the parents I wanted. What next? Well, I guess I'll find out tomorrow, won't I, with Door 3 coming right up.

Jenna made her way out of the room, gave it one last glance, and closed the door. She went back to her temporary bedroom, took out a piece of paper, and wrote a poem before going to sleep, exhausted after everything she'd experienced in Door 2.

All the emotion and remembering was bringing back her poetic creativity.

Compassion.
Love.
Fear.
Unease.

Four words that shouldn't go together.
Idilic times versus stormy weather.

Why can't we have just the top two?
Why do we have to muddle through?

I mourn what I didn't have as a child.
I guess I deserved it for being a wild child.

But was I that person they said I was?
Surely I didn't have all those flaws?

Self-compassion is hard,
When you haven't been taught it.

Compassion is a reward
I can only give myself.

Lick the wounds of the past,
And make sure you heal them fast.

They'll haunt me 'til I die,
And sometimes they'll still make me cry.

Love will win every time,
Wherever it comes from.
It must start from inside.

CHAPTER 4

The Unknown

Not knowing
It gets to the best of us.
Will we reap the seeds we're sowing?

Searching for knowledge
Searching for Truth.
I'm on the fence, right on the edge,
I wish I could get back to the naivety of my youth.

No need for anything
Just rely on existing day by day.
Enjoying the back and forth on my swing
Gently I just sway and sway.

No more of that though
I had to grow up.
Get on with it, stop feeling so low,
Hide those tears with some makeup…

It is the fear of the unknown
The doubts that have been sown.
In these poems I hide,
Until all those doubts are tried.

Not knowing,
It's a way of life.
Not knowing,
Carrying on through the strife...

*R*oom 3! she exclaimed as she woke up, realising she was still in that strange place. She mused on how funny it was when people were sleeping or near waking they could imagine themselves anywhere. Maybe it was hotel from a fun holiday or in a favourite bedroom that was taken away suddenly by the so-called need to move to a better place ...

What's wrong with this place? As she gathered her early morning thoughts over some cheese and toast, she recalled the poem she wrote about the unknowns and having to grow up and carry on with life in spite of those "seeds of doubt" her upbringing and the real world had enveloped her with.

That wasn't that long ago; I still feel a bit like that. Lots of things I still don't know, and I can't imagine figuring some of those out, ever. I guess that's what life is like, right? But why? I don't want to walk around not knowing.

Jenna stared at her music box while her thoughts wandered. It was shiny and not dusty anymore, like it was brand new. It started playing an eerie sounding song. *Geez, if you could put a tune to how I'm feeling—all this not knowing—this would be exactly it. Man, this box is freaking me out. Better get to Room 3 before it starts going berserk!*

As Jenna walked to the doors, she was feeling a bit nervous. Her heart was beating faster, and her breath grew shallower. She hadn't had this much in the previous rooms; it had been more "thinky" there. But this room was different somehow. *Maybe because it's the third room? What's going to happen when I go in there?*

Jenna decided to just go for it. She didn't even sit down in front of the door to contemplate it until she felt brave enough.

It was now or never—*although never might mean never leaving this place, so that's not an option anyway. Ah well, here we go.*

At first glance, the room was quite ordinary. It didn't shock Jenna or do much to her. It was familiar but also new. The things she'd found in the other rooms—things from her past—weren't there. The walls looked like they were covered in striped wallpaper, but as she got closer, she noticed there was tiny writing on the walls.

On closer inspection, she realised that each line had a different word. Some were brighter than others. *Why are they brighter, these ones here? Am I supposed to focus on those?* As she thought that, the music box played an upbeat tune as if to say, "Bingo, you got it!".

KNOWLEDGE
INTENSITY
SOW THE SEEDS
CONFIDENCE
EMPOWERMENT
TRUST
TRUTH

Those words looked shinier and brighter on the walls. *Now, what in the world am I supposed to . . . Oh! Look at that! It looks like a dictionary, but it's only got some words in it, not a usual dictionary at all. But nothing is usual about this place. No surprises there, I guess.*

Jenna approached the book with curiosity. As she opened it, she realised the words written in it were the same ones on the wall. *Well, that's just extra strange. Take me back to the first two rooms, please.* She thought it a bit sarcastically but with a twinge of fear in her internal voice.

Although it was all a bit weird, and she wasn't sure what that room was about, Jenna was at least relieved to see that they were all positive and hopeful sounding words, unlike Room

1 and 2, where it was an emotional rollercoaster through the stuff she'd endured growing up. *Is this pointing me towards the future? If so, I'm intrigued.*

As she was reading, Jenna knew she'd better pay attention, or she might never get out of that place. What if the room was about teaching her things that would help her in the future? She wouldn't want to miss those, would she?

Knowledge is interesting, she thought. *It's very true; there's a lot not known.* Jenna continued reading and pondering. It helped her understand and retain the information a bit better. It was a technique she discovered at university. *It would've been helpful in school, but hey, better late than never.*

Jenna read a sentence from the book. "True knowledge comes from within." *That's interesting. I thought it came from books and what my teachers taught me. I guess, as this says, knowing myself, what I like and don't like, what my boundaries are, and what I need to be happy, is more important than what we can learn from others or books.*

Harnessing the power we have as humans sounds a bit dangerous. If it's is discovered by the wrong people, what can we do to prevent them from using it in the wrong way?

Free will? Free thinking? Free feeling? Who wrote this thing? She kept reading:

We would be able to engage with our Creator in a more direct and palpable way. We limit ourselves when we say "I don't know enough" or "I should've known that." Humans have been conditioned to say these things to themselves. We are conditioned to think that if we say we're knowledgeable at something or good at something, we're selfish or arrogant. Knowledge isn't haughty. Knowledge isn't for sale. Knowledge is free and easy to find if we just look inward and nurture what's already there. Knowledge is rooted in our beings. It is the essence of who we are. We were created in God's image, and if God has all the knowledge, and we're His children, then so do we.

Ok, I like that. This room is all about knowledge—or not knowing. I'm not sure anymore, but let's make it positive; I've had enough negative the last couple of days with the whole journey to the past I'd buried. So, if I think about what this is saying, what I should be doing is looking inward for knowledge. Maybe it's a bit of both? I can get knowledge from others, but ultimately, it's up to me what I choose to do with the information I get from them and how I integrate it into my own life, right? Jenna reveled in the happier music coming from the music box and knew she was on the right track.

Anyway. I like that part about having been conditioned. If we can be conditioned one way, surely, we can be re-conditioned (is that a word?) in another direction. Let's try this out. Mum used to say, "Just get on with it." How can I change that into something kinder, something I can roll with? Maybe something like "Sit with it, deal with it, then move on with your life." Yes! That feels much better. Jenna smiled as she realized she would be happy to say that to anyone and that it sat well within her.

What's next? Intensity. Ok, a definition of intensity. Well, well, well, that's interesting! I was told that I was too intense growing up, that I should "pipe down a notch or two." The synonyms are ringing true for me; I wasn't too much, I didn't need to pipe down. I was passionate and enthusiastic and blatantly misunderstood by the parentals. The antonyms definitely and completely describe them—insensitive and impassive or apathetic. Gosh, this little gem is wonderful! The more Jenna read, the more confident and happy she became. She mused about how scared she'd been going into the room, but somehow, it felt magical.

The third phrase was "sow the seeds." Jenna took her time to read through that one, taking a few deep breaths. It felt like she was being freed of something—many things, actually—as she went through what that room had to offer her.

Sometimes, we might feel like our words hit walls instead of interested ears, like what we say, feel, or think isn't relevant. The thing is, we never know who we're reaching with our words or when those things we said will take root and start to grow. If you've ever been to therapy, you'll know what this is like. Sowing seeds, whether in therapy or daily life, through reading or talking to someone, will affect you in one way or another. Sooner or later. Trust that. Keep planting seeds and wait for them to grow. It's magical!

Gosh, that first line really got me. Where are the tissues? That's exactly how I felt when I was trying to talk to my parents. She paused to consider how different that was from the dream she had in the room the day before. *I have never gone to therapy, but I'll certainly consider it after this. A-ha moments sound great.* Jenna had quite a few of those moments in the strange house. She'd uncovered parts of herself she'd hidden or forgotten. *Maybe there's more locked in there that needs to come out—hopefully, I don't wake up in a stranger's house with my stuff in it again. I still don't get it, but here we are. Sow seeds. Keep sowing seeds in myself and others. Trust in the seeds. Lovely! What's next?*

When we start to accept who we are, warts and all (and we all have them, in varying sizes and colours), we start to recognise the greatness that's within us.

Ok, ok, ok, stop it now, book! I am getting the drift of your message. Confidence. I need to be more confident. I guess with the knowledge and intensity or passion spiel I just read, I can gain some of that confidence that it's talking about.

If Jenna was truthful with herself, she realised she wasn't feeling very confident after experiencing the other rooms. *Trust is the next label. Kept this one short and sweet, huh?*

Trust comes after I just say I'm not feeling confident! Oh, you're clever, Mr. Magical Book! Let's see if I can answer your questions.

"How do we trust when we've been told we're untrustworthy?" *Uhm, well, it goes with having confidence in oneself, as it says on the previous page, as well as knowing that I'm good enough. People seem to like me, to hang around me, to invite me to parties and things. I probably just need to find some more evidence in my life that backs up the fact that I'm trustworthy.* Jenna was shocked about where the insight came from. *This little book is rubbing off on me.*

"How do we trust when those who were meant to look after us let us down?" *Geez, that's a hard one. I guess I developed a lack of trust from having grown up with parents who let me down a lot.* She remembered that scene where she saw through the window in the second room where she couldn't hug her friend's parents at first, but a few visits later, she was happy to embrace them and felt very welcome by them. *Ok, I guess people make themselves trustworthy. Is that it? Also, it might be about me feeling they are trustworthy. I'll keep thinking about this one; it's a heavy one!*

Own your truth.
Trust in your truth.
Explore it and act accordingly.
It's the nicest thing you can do for yourself!

The last one was difficult for Jenna. *What's my truth? How do I trust my truth? I have no clue. I'm so used to comparing what I know and feel with what other people know and feel that trusting things without comparison or checking will be tricky. What works for me? Who the heck knows! I know what doesn't work for me, but I don't know what to do with it. I guess this is a work in progress, and I'll just have to see about that when I get back home—if I ever get back home, that is.*

As she sat there, reading and re-reading the little book of magical information, Jenna felt more and more encouraged and soothed. She felt like hugging herself, so she wrapped her arms around her chest and squeezed tightly.

It was several hours before her normal bedtime, so Jenna decided to go back to the other rooms since she'd found some renewed strength through the third room and its contents. She didn't want to brush things under the carpet anymore. She knew what this had done to her in the past, making her feel isolated and burdensome. It had taken a lot for her to realise she hadn't dealt with any of this in a long time. Finally, she accepted how freeing it felt to have opened the three mysterious doors and looked inside.

Jenna was still confused about what was happening, but she couldn't escape it either. What she'd done over those few days was brave. Exploring a whole new world, with a wealth of memories—many painful, others bittersweet—and other very lovely ones hadn't been that bad.

Well, bumping my head on the first morning here wasn't the best. A baffling start! It's actually turning out to be quite nice. I hope I wake up here tomorrow morning. I can't wait to see if there are any more rooms in this house to explore!

Before bedtime, she wrote another poem about her experiences in room 3.

Answers

I have searched and searched,
And found some answers.

I have cried and cried,
And stood up once I was done.

I grew up,
I reconciled with my past and myself.

I began a journey,
That will never end.

I know more now,
Than I did then.

But that doesn't mean that
Not knowing will end.

JEREMIAH

JEREMIAH

CHAPTER 5

Meet Your Match

Jeremiah woke up, barely aware of his surroundings. Barely aware was the understatement of the year. *Man! What a night. I've never drunk that much in my life.* He knew that wasn't true. He often consumed many drinks, and last night wasn't any different.

In the back of his mind, he knew he needed to sort himself out—in the very, very, very back of his mind. In reality, he had no intention of being "serious" anytime soon.

I really need the toilet! Where are my glasses? He reached over to his night table, and when he realised there was nothing there, it was too late. He tumbled out and found the floor a few seconds later, with a great *thud*.

Urgh! What the . . . Hey! What's going on here? How did I fall so far down? My bed isn't that high off the floor. He assessed his pains and then somehow found his glasses. Once his eyes adjusted to the bit of light seeping through the half-closed curtains, he suddenly became extremely nervous.

Uhm . . . Jeremiah looked at the bunk bed he fell from with confusion. *This isn't my room. But that's my blanket, that's my stuff . . . but no, wait. That's old stuff! How much did I drink? Even worse, what did I drink?! I don't remember alcohol doing this to me. Oh, my head hurts. I need medicine. I need sleep. Maybe I can go back to sleep. Am I still dreaming?*

The questions came quickly through his aching head. He couldn't answer a single one of them.Jeremiah pinched himself, and the pain he'd inflicted upon himself was so real it confirmed he was indeed awake and undeniably somewhere he'd never been before.

Jeremiah started to get agitated. Not his usual agitation; this was fear. This was scary. This was beyond bizarre! *Oh my God, oh my God! I need to get out of here!*

Here . . . where is here? "Hello?" he called out. *I don't remember falling asleep in this room.* He knew he couldn't possibly have climbed up that ladder in his intoxicated state. *I would have happily lied down in the corner on the floor than attempt a ladder like that!*

He went to the window to try and open it, but it seemed jammed. He exhausted himself trying to open it. After around ten minutes of attempting it, he decided he'd give up. *Giving up. Well, that's an interesting choice of words. Although not unexpected, given my current predicament.* He knew he didn't have time to dwell on it too long, so he decided to explore the strange room.

The house appeared to be a refurbished barn. He could see the repainted old wood and the newer materials that replaced some of the tired old planks of wood on the walls. *Rustic.*

Where am I? And why's my stuff here? He knew it was all his, but he hadn't seen any of it since before his family moved to a new house when he was seventeen.

A notebook caught his attention. *That's my old journal! I haven't written since my mum found it and read it. She was always so nosey! I thought I threw that out ages ago.* When he grabbed it, he instantly felt a wave of emotions hit him—all kinds of emotions he was still too drunk to process.

Jeremiah quickly dropped the notebook and scowled. *This isn't normal. Where the hell am I? How did I end up here?* He massaged his throbbing temples and considered it might be more than a hangover. He'd sobered up quite a bit since his fall from the bunk bed.

The need to use the toilet interrupted his thinking. The thought of leaving this room stopped him in his tracks for more than one reason. First, he needed to find the toilet. He had an ensuite back home, but this room didn't have any other doors than the one he was staring at, wondering and fearing the worst.

Second, the fact that there wasn't an ensuite meant that he'd have to leave the room. Was he safe? Opening the door could mean his demise.

His urge to pee got the best of Jeremiah. He wasn't that careful anyway and being slightly drunk still, he thought he would chance it and open the door. Reassuring himself, he hoped he would find someone who could explain everything but was also hoping that person wasn't a murderer.

Stop it. Stop thinking like that. What good is that gonna do? Just open the door and see if you can get out another way. He listened for a few seconds, then opened the door in one swift move. Silence. Nobody was there. He stood there for what felt an eternity.

Jeremiah gazed around, taking in the scene. He was downstairs. It was an open-floorplan layout, so the lounge and kitchen were visible from where he was standing. Taking in all the colour, brightness, and quietness of the room, he felt reassured that nothing terrible and torturous was about to happen to him. He looked upstairs and noticed three doors.

Within seconds, his arm prinkled with goosebumps. Emotions overwhelmed him once more, and he felt sobriety wash over him. *Right. Toilet. Run for it and lock yourself there while you do your business. You're going to burst and hurt yourself if you don't go now!*

He made it to the bathroom and relieved himself. It was a good-sized bathroom with country-style furniture and bath in it, which he thought he might use later if he didn't find anyone else around. Jeremiah had no idea how long he was even going to be there.

I might as well enjoy myself while I'm here, right? He suspected that the journal was a clue—and he wasn't going to enjoy it. *I don't want to, but at the same time, I really want to read that journal again.*

Jeremiah had written so much in those pages. He would rather forget what was in them. Those years weren't pleasant for him. In fact, those years were what led him to drink. It was weird for him to think like that, but it was true. Even though it was years ago, he still thought about that time in his life. He shivered just thinking about it.

If I was at home, I'd be getting my protein shake out of the fridge right about now. That always makes me feel better after a night like last night. I can't imagine they have that here.

They? Who are they?

He went to the kitchen, got himself a drink—not his protein shake, but it wasn't too bad, and found pain killers. With nothing else to do in the kitchen—and he didn't dare think about the three freaky doors up the stairs—he went back to the room he woke up in and closed the door behind him, checking the front door before he went. *Of course, it's locked.*

At least he knew he was alone. He wasn't sure that was a good thing yet.

Jeremiah decided he knew enough now about the house to sit down and think. No, he needed to let the pain killers kick in first. He was in no fit state to think sensibly yet. *Not that I ever have,* he thought.

Jeremiah sat down in a chair. *Comfy!* He was reminded of the journal, which was lying on the floor right in front of him. He picked it up, and an overwhelming surge of emotions tore through his whole being. The sensation caused him to drop the book, which fell open to a drawing he'd made when he was ten.

It reminded Jeremiah of the day his mum confronted him about the journal. He knew why he'd drawn that picture and written what was on those pages. *I can't believe my mum read that and saw my pictures! She never listened to me. She didn't respect me back then and still doesn't now.*

He thought he'd buried those feelings deep down. So deep, they had no chance of rising again. But there he was, feeling like that ten-year-old version of himself he thought he'd left behind.

The memories were fleeting, but the emotions attached to them were powerful. *I don't want to think about what happened that year. I don't want to feel like this, especially in this strange house.*

Jeremiah wondered about the strange rooms upstairs, too. *I've never had such strong emotions from just staring at a set of doors before. I don't understand what's going on here.* He felt overwhelmingly vulnerable and wanted to curl up on the floor and rock himself to sleep like he'd done when younger.

He wasn't sure it safe, though, to fall asleep. There was concern about what he'd wake up to or whether he'd even wake up if he slept. *How did I get moved here without knowing about it? I mean, I did drink a heck of a lot last night, but even I know better than to go home with someone I don't know or alone and turn up in a strange house like this one. Of all the stupid things I've done in the past few years, I never expected to end up in a strange house in an unknown place!*

He shifted in his seat and kicked the journal with his foot. As it closed itself back up and made that distinctive noise old books make when shut, Jeremiah realised there was a similarity between the sensation the rooms upstairs gave him and how his journal and the memories they were summoning made him feel.

Jeremiah couldn't pinpoint what the emotions he felt were. He never could. How could he? He had no point of reference. He just knew it wasn't comfortable to feel that way.

Somewhere in his mind, he also knew that to get out of this house, he'd have to face what was in that journal and possibly what he'd find in those three rooms upstairs.

He glanced around at some of his stuff in this room and wondered what on earth could possibly be waiting for him upstairs. There weren't many options in his current predicament. He could stay there forever, or he could go and see what was behind those three doors upstairs and hope to get out of there sooner than later. *Well*, he thought, *investigating what is going on with these rooms and this house, and me waking up in this house, seems like the lesser of two evils right now.*

CHAPTER 6

Whirlwind

JOURNAL ENTRY, May 7, 1995

Well, she's done it again. I don't know how she does it, but whatever she does, it always comes to haunt me. Me! Why me? I don't understand why she's like that with me. I know I have "anger issues," as I'm constantly reminded, but that doesn't mean I don't have any other feelings. I get hurt. I cry. I never show anyone, but I cry. I guess I don't like being misunderstood or people thinking things of me that I know aren't true.

As Jeremiah read that bit of his journal, he remembered how his mum used to stay in bed a lot of the time when he was growing up. His dad was never there; he didn't even remember his face—that's how long it had been since he saw him. Dad had become a silhouette of a man in his memories. There, but not at all there, either. He didn't understand what was wrong with his mum, but how she acted around him made him feel like it was his fault.

I wonder how different life might have been if I had known my father. My mum couldn't look after herself. She was upset all the time. I couldn't ask her for anything because she'd get so angry. I just wanted something to eat or show her my drawings, but that was obviously too much for her. Ugh!

As he thought that, Jeremiah realised he'd been gripping onto the side of the chair really hard and ripped a bit of the old fabric off. It was a green sofa with that itchy material that his grandma's blankets used to have. Uncomfortable, but at the same time, familiar. *Wait, this is Grandma's chair! I used to love sitting in it with her when I was little. Those were some of the only times I felt at peace and like I wasn't doing anything wrong. I guess growing up wasn't all that bad after all. Silver linings, huh?*

As he sat there, contemplating his time with his grandmother, he turned the pages of his journal and stumbled across one of his drawings. It was different than the one before. *Strange.* On the page, he'd drawn a large door with a huge key in it. It was dark brown—*similar to those weird freaky doors outside, now that I think about it*—and looked extremely heavy for a regular household door. *What was I thinking when I drew that? Well, did I actually draw that?* He checked his other drawings and noticed the doors he drew were flat and thin, not massive like the one he was looking at with eerie attention.

He noticed different colors around the door, particularly greys and reds—both signifying gloom and aggression or anger. The drawing, which he still wasn't sure he'd drawn, drew Jeremiah in with every swirl of colour. It was like the hues were coming out from behind the door, a mystery still to Jeremiah.

Ah, ok. This place is some kind of a magical place, right? He knew that seemed insane but couldn't think of any other explanation. Jeremiah hadn't found signs of anyone else in the house, he didn't know how he got there, and his stuff from his childhood was waiting in the room for him to find. *Some of this stuff my mum threw away a long time ago.*

As Jeremiah finished his thought, he got up and made his way to the bedroom door. There was a brief moment of hesitation before he opened it. He specifically avoided looking at the doors upstairs; they freaked him out. With a deep breath, he recalled the drawing of the door that had light shining out of it. He'd painted with those same angry, dark colours lots of times. They weren't comforting, but they were certainly accurate.

I can do this. Jeremiah stood, staring at the floor for a long time. He took a deep breath in and started to walk up the stairs quickly before he could change his mind and wimp out. *Wimp out. Ouch! Mum used to say that to me all the time. "Are you going to wimp out again, son? It's not that hard; just do it!"* Those words still stung.

He looked at his journal and found the door that looked the most like the one in the drawing—it was strange how the three were identical, but at the same time, there was something very different about each one. It's as if their aura—*if that's even a real thing,* he thought—was different and displaying different hues of colour to his unconscious eye.

After a few moments of holding his hand mid-air near the door handle but far enough to feel safe, he decided to open it.

As Jeremiah opened the door, ever so slowly, he started to notice and recognise the walls. He used to get in trouble for drawing on them, but he didn't care; it was cathartic for him, and it was his room anyway, right?

Just as in the drawing, he noticed he used a lot of red and grey tones. *It must've been some kind of display of how I was feeling. Unfortunately, I was misunderstood and called a mess.* To young Jeremiah, it was art. It was his company when he felt lonely. *I remember adding more strokes as each day passed.* There was one that caught his eye, the one he added the day his mum told him his grandma had died, and they weren't going to attend her funeral. *I was so sad but also so angry at her. I loved my grandma. She knew that, yet she denied me saying goodbye to her like everyone else was able to do.*

• • •

The journal was sitting in Jeremiah's grandmother's chair, which had mysteriously appeared in the room. The journal would occasionally turn to a different page, making Jeremiah jump. He was startled by the movement, especially since he knew he was absolutely on his own.

Jeremiah walked around the room, exploring the walls and the writing he'd done on them. Memories continued to come up for him with each phrase, word, colour he used. His whole body kept shifting, shaking, recoiling at the emotions that accompanied each of those marks on the walls.

The first sentences Jeremiah came across made him scrunch up his face. As he looked at the bright red and purple hues mixing, making some darker tones at certain points, he realised that he was extremely upset when he wrote it.

Does anyone deserve what they get? Is there a point to being punished like this?

When did I write that? I must've been grounded or something. Maybe it was on the day of grandma's funeral. I still don't understand why I wasn't allowed to go. Maybe that's why her chair is there? Am I angry with mum? I can't possibly be upset with grandma, right?

While he thought that, a soft breeze shifted the journal to an entry dated on the day of his grandmother's funeral:

July 27, 1997

Grandma's funeral is today. I am not allowed to go. I don't understand. I want to say goodbye to her.

Grandma! Why did you have to die and leave me here with these people? Why couldn't they go and you stay here and make me smile and laugh, and listen to my crazy stories and ideas?

Why is life so unfair? Why do I have to go through this on my own? What have I done that's so bad that I am being punished like this?

It's her fault, she didn't look after herself so well, and now she's dead. What am I supposed to do now? I guess I'm destined to a pathetic, sorry life, without much laughter and with nobody to talk to.

Grandma, I hate that you left me. I hate that you didn't fight to stay alive longer.

I hate that I'm left here all on my own, with that woman who thinks everything I do is wrong and how I should know better about everything.

Jeremiah sat down and stared at the journal for what felt to him like an eternity. When he came out of his daze, he realised tears were running down his face. He wasn't sure if they were sad tears or angry tears but probably more the latter. He mostly cried out of anger growing up, which seemed to have been the norm for him. *Mum would respond to the anger but not to the sadness.*

As Jeremiah felt his way through his memories, a rage he'd thought he'd long left behind overtook him. It felt like it enveloped every cell of his body; he clenched his hands so tightly he'd made himself bleed as his nails dug deep into his skin. He was frustrated by the flashbacks to a time he didn't want to revisit but was being forced to by the writing on the wall and the journal entries.

● ● ●

He spent a long while pondering the flashbacks, memories, and the anger he felt back then. When Jeremiah was wiping away unexpected tears, a strong wind engulfed the whole room. It was like a whirlwind, almost tornado-like. He grabbed hold of his grandmother's chair and crouched in it like he did when he was a child before his grandma came to join him to read and rock him to sleep.

The whirlwind sounded angry. It whistled violently into Jeremiah's ear, swooshing back and forth throughout the room. The wind rustled his journal pages, and everything that wasn't too heavy in the room took on a life of his own. Jeremiah thought one of the airborne items might hit him, but they didn't. *Phew.* He felt the whirlwind was shouting with rage at him, like it was taunting him, telling him that he should feel angry—as angry as the wind itself. From behind his arms, which were working as shields from the wind that seemed to be attacking him, he saw the words he'd written years ago, in reds and greys, swirl around in thin air, all around the room:

"Does anyone deserve what they get?"
"Is there a point to being punished like this?"
"I hate this life. Why am I even here?"
"I must be an awful person to be treated like this."
"Hate."
"Anger."
"Rage."
"Die or murder."

Those last few letters shocked him to the core. He had forgotten he wrote those two words—die or murder. As he recognised them, the wind intensified for a few seconds and then, in the same way as it began, it stopped altogether, leaving the room in complete, unnerving silence.

As Jeremiah gathered himself, calming himself with deep breaths and hoping that the strong wind wouldn't come back. He said, "Ok, I get it. Please don't attack again. I know what to do now."

While he spoke those words, he noticed his old journal had opened up to a blank page. A pen rolled off the dresser and made Jeremiah jump. He picked it up, still shaking from all that he had just experienced and from the tears he'd shed remembering all of the things surrounding his grandmother's death.

Jeremiah took a deep breath and started writing . . .

JOURNAL ENTRY, November 17, 2018

Hi, old friend. I guess I'm in the place where all my thoughts went. Old habits die hard in this place, wherever this is. I really don't know what to write. I still don't understand what's going on.

I look at the walls around me and shudder at the memory of how deadly my anger was back then. I say "back then," but I can still feel it bubbling inside me now. How have I got this far without dealing with it?

Has this been the key in my issues with my teachers, my sort of girlfriends, my boss, my friends, with myself even?

That whirlwind . . . that's how this feels, that is how it felt back then. I don't like it.

I didn't like it then, but I didn't know how to stop. Well, that's not completely right; maybe all the scribbling on the wall was my way of preventing some of the anger from coming out in ways that I don't even want to think about!

But do I have it in me to kill myself or to commit murder? I hope not!

I haven't done it in all my years of being alive and keeping this in, but the rage was so huge, I can probably see how people get themselves into those positions—either taking their own or someone else's life.

I'm rambling! Dammit, it's my diary. I'll ramble all I want!

So what's next? I have two more rooms to explore in this house. I can't imagine what will be in them after the literal whirlwind this room has been.

I've just tried to open the door, but it won't budge. I guess I'm not finished with whatever is going on in this room.

Anger.

Let's deal with it then so I can get out of here.

Signing out for now . . .

As Jeremiah pondered on the anger and on the words he'd just written in his journal, he knew what he needed to do. He'd noticed some cleaning products in the corner and cloths to use with them. He picked them up and started cleaning the writing on the wall. He read each sentence as he did and remembered the scenes that led him to write each one. As he erased each phrase from the wall, he could see the white of the original wall.

Jeremiah worked on erasing the words for what seemed an eternity. Tears flowed freely down his face, and his grip tightened on the cloth as he worked through all the anger he'd stashed deep inside his unconscious for so many years. As hard as it was, it was also freeing. He felt the grip of rage release slowly as he went through the whole room. When he finished, he found himself in a room that had no trace of anger anymore.

He had dealt with it.

Well, I had no choice, the door is locked, and obviously, this is what I needed to do. It feels right. It didn't when I walked in, but I can see clearer now. I feel like I can understand my mother a bit now, even though what she did still hurts and will hurt forever. I can forgive her for not being able to be the mother I needed her to be. I can forgive my grandmother for leaving me. I really hope to see her again sometime soon!

Jeremiah wasn't sure he was done dealing with this past. He felt a lot more anger swirling inside. *Maybe the next room will tell me. This is so weird, a room telling me things? What's going on?*

CHAPTER 7

The Darkest Depths

Jeremiah stayed in the room, pondering the question, "What's going on?" until late in the evening. He left the room, almost in a daze, and somehow made it back into the bedroom. He was so exhausted. After all, he'd just had a literal whirlwind in that first room, but he had done so nursing a terrible hangover. As he tried to fall asleep, he couldn't help but think about his grandmother's laughter and his mother lying in her bed, unwell. It took him a while before he drifted off into a deep sleep. That night, his unconscious mind put on a great show for him. He didn't remember them, but his jaw was aching when he awoke, a sign he had been clenching it tightly through the night.

Jeremiah woke up feeling unsettled, slightly wary of what the day's room would bring, and somewhat unsure that what happened the day before wasn't a dream.

As Jeremiah walked out of the room and went toward the kitchen, he looked at the doors. "The angry door," as he named it, looked very unseemly and almost irrelevant. If it weren't for what he went through in there, he'd even call it unimportant. Despite the door's plainness, his experiences in the room made him feel strangely connected to it.

Instead of the red and grey hues emanating from the gaps in the door, normal daylight was seeping through—sort of what happens after a storm: calm is restored, and you can almost hear the silence and peace amongst the disaster left behind.

That's how Jeremiah felt, like he'd wrecked the place inside himself. For so many years, it was the place where, due to his circumstances, he'd chosen to deal with or avoid them. The whirlwind felt like a reenactment of his repressed emotions, wreaking havoc from the beyond, from the deepest, most hidden parts of his mind and heart. Erasing those phrases didn't give him amnesia—*oh no, no amnesia here. I can still remember everything.* Erasing those phrases on the wall, written in rage, led him to feel what he hadn't felt for so long, even those things he didn't realise were there. And now he wondered what was next.

• • •

Jeremiah had something to eat from the oddly very well-stocked kitchen. *Thank you, whoever you are, for knowing what my favourite breakfast foods are now and what they were growing up.* It was very reassuring to him, somehow, even though he still had no idea where he was.

After breakfast, Jeremiah washed his plate and cup and walked towards the second door, which was emitting a spectrum of blue lights. He started thinking about the difference between the red and grey hues from "the angry door" versus the blue hues in this second door, yet to be named.

What the heck, let's go in and face this one; it can't possibly be as bad as the angry one! Jeremiah paused to contemplate that thought. He wondered how rooms could hold specific emotions and how they could provoke emotions on someone inside. *Does it just work on me?*

As he was about to step forward and open the door, Jeremiah recalled how enlightening his journal had been in the previous room. While he hadn't written in one for years, he had to admit it was therapeutic to get his thoughts on paper the day prior. He dashed downstairs and grabbed the notebook from his temporary bedroom.

When he returned to the door, he paused and stared at the doorknob for a few minutes, gathering strength and getting excited and anxious all at once. Jeremiah fell to his knees when he opened the door, overwhelmed by something so powerful, he had to remember to breathe before he passed out. It was almost like he'd been hit in the stomach but not quite the same. It was as if his whole body crumbled under some invisible pressure. He was only halfway in the room when he collapsed. He decided that getting up would be futile, so he crawled into the middle of the room.

This room was very different. There was a spotlight on him, and everything else was dim. Jeremiah could hardly see the walls. In fact, he noticed the room was mostly empty and bigger than it should've been, given the dimensions of the actual house. *But what do I know? If I can wake up in this place, and have feelings come up with each room, with everything I touch here, then I guess the dimensions can also be altered to fit whatever the purpose of this second room is. If anyone is watching or listening to my thoughts, they probably think I've lost the plot!*

Jeremiah wished he was still drunk as he faced this new room. At the same time, he pondered what the point would be if he was drunk. Would he have to repeat the experience if he was not fully aware whilst going into the rooms? *They— whoever "they" are—would just make me go through it again, with my full capacity. Have I ever had that?*

Lost in thought, Jeremiah noticed a second spotlight shone on his journal. His eyebrow went up as a spooky feeling arose in his gut; goosebumps on his arms and a shudder shook him back into his present predicament. He'd gone into a bit of a daze, void of thought, where nothing was of consequence. It was a skill he'd developed growing up when curling up on the floor and falling asleep wouldn't help. *Dissociation?*

Somebody he knew had said that's what it sounded like. Regardless of what it was called, it helped Jeremiah disengage from everything, even if it didn't last long. His mum would inevitably shout and bring him back to the moment.

He guessed that this is why drinking had become a coping mechanism for him—he could disengage from things as he got himself into a drunken stupor. The problem with this was the moral hangover—and the physical hangover, of course—he felt the day after.

Let's do this. Sober, but what the heck. Maybe it's time I faced things without that wretched stuff. I know it's bad for me, but it's also a friend.

JOURNAL ENTRY, October 1998

I had my first drink yesterday and really liked it. Screwdrivers are the best. Was it vodka and orange juice? It must have been. I don't know what happened after that. I don't know how I got home, but here I am, writing in my journal, so I must've made it back somehow.

I'm feeling a bit woozy right now, but I'm sure it will pass. I wonder if I did anything stupid last night?

Oh no, what if I spoke to that girl I like and made a complete fool of myself?

I don't want to know. I'm sure my friends will let me know what happened when we meet again. What have I done?

UPDATE: Apparently, I didn't do anything that stupid, but I did zone out for a long time, which worried Mike and Joe. They said they were about to call 999, but I suddenly snapped out of it and got up and went home.

As he stared at the journal entry, he remembered it like it was yesterday. He didn't remember where he went for the time he'd zoned out but thought how it must've felt nice. It meant he wasn't aware of his distress or his anger—everything he had to live through with his ill mum. *I can see now how and when I started using drink to stop the sadness.*

As he thought the word "sadness," he realised how the melancholy had become extremely tangible in the room: heavy, overwhelming, oppressive, and overpowering. The sensations made him fall forward from his seated position, his face pressed against the floor.

Jeremiah realised he'd been lying on the floor for a while and started crying—sobbing like he hadn't since he was little. As he cried, he felt a wave of memories come toward him. Particularly, he remembered the day he was told his grandmother had died and the day of the funeral.

He recalled the anger he felt at his mother for denying him the right to say goodbye. He also remembered the emptiness he felt during those days.

Since he wasn't allowed to attend, Jeremiah took himself to the far end of his garden on the day of the funeral. He sat there all day until his mum dragged him indoors around midnight. She wasn't aware of how he felt, and he didn't feel like he could tell her. He would only get the same response as always: shouting and a complete disregard of his feelings and thoughts. As always, his mum wasn't available to meet his emotional needs. She wasn't even available to meet her own emotional needs. Jeremiah had never thought of it that way until he re-read those familiar words she'd say to him—he'd recorded them in his journal.

"Stop being such a baby!"
"You'll be fine; just don't think about it."
"Don't be such a wimp!"
"There's nothing you can do about it."

"I'm going to go lie down, don't get yourself into trouble."

It seemed to help him get those thoughts out of his head, but it also made them more tangible. In spite of having heard them from her own mouth, acknowledging them as real made things harder for him.

And so the emptiness and sadness took over. Mix that up with the anger, and there's a great recipe for hopelessness, for the despair Jeremiah usually felt and tried to hide from through drinking.

But he was sober now. Jeremiah sat and stared into the dark space, eyes full of shock and surreal sensations he had numbed for so long. In this darkened room, heavy with all kinds of memories flashing through his mind, he had to acknowledge it all.

Sadness wasn't something he wanted to face. But he had no other choice anymore. It was difficult to sit in the dark, empty room, which accurately represented how he'd felt on and off throughout his life, culminating with the loss of his grandmother.

He decided to lose himself in his journal again. It had been helpful in the past and proved useful again the day before in "the angry room."

JOURNAL ENTRY, November 18, 2018

The whole experience in this room has been surreal—even more than the anger one. The nothingness, the emptiness of this room is very eerily noisy, in spite of it being completely quiet in here.

I know I felt this when Grandma died. It still feels like yesterday, even though it was twenty years ago. I miss her so much. She didn't know everything that went on with mum, but she didn't need to. She loved me, no matter what.

Oops, my tears are making these pages soggy. Aw well, what can I do? Better get this out, or I might stay in this empty space forever.

What's with these rooms, this house, this whole experience that's making me face my deepest, darkest, mostly forgotten (maybe repressed is a better word) memories and emotions?

Well, I say emotions, but I'm realising more and more that I didn't really feel these at the time. How could I? I was always told not to be a wimp or think about things.

I don't know. Maybe being told that was what made me get on the drink as hard as I did. Will I still want to drink after this? When I get back home, whenever, however that will happen, will I be able not to drink, or just drink socially rather than drink myself stupid every given opportunity?

I guess recognising drinking was what was keeping all of these emotions and memories from surfacing and having felt these things now—and still one room to go!—will I be different, or will it be the same old Jeremiah who can't get his life straight?

Maybe I can stop talking about myself to myself in such an awful way?

I don't know. I just feel so empty right now. What do I need to do to get rid of this sadness? I know yesterday I erased the angry words I'd written on the wall, but I don't know if today will work similarly. There's nothing in this room!

As Jeremiah wrote those final words in his journal, a light shone from the wall. He realised it was something like a tv screen. What he saw made him jump up and get very close to the screen, like he had when he was a child.

He saw his grandmother sitting in the same chair he'd been sitting in yesterday. Tears pooled in his eyes. She looked so happy. But when was this? Where was this? It wasn't her house. It wasn't this house either. Where was she?

Jeremiah realised his grandmother was saying something. He stopped his racing thoughts and tried hard to listen.

"My dearest child, I know you miss me. I'm so sorry I left you like that. I wish you'd been there to say your final goodbye to me. But trust that I came to see you and give you a final kiss before heading to my final destination, where I'll see you when it's your time to join me. I wish I could've been there to tell you everything would be ok, and your mother was wrong to treat you like she did. I'd like to say she didn't know better, but that would only be a little bit true—what she did still hurt, and excusing or explaining her behaviour her won't change that. Make sure you forgive her, though, because it will only hurt you not to. It's for your benefit, not hers. I hope you can find the peace, reassurance, and strength to carry on with your life. You are great just as you are. Find your path and stick with it. I love you, my grandson."

He couldn't hold back his tears. How could this be? How did this happen? Jeremiah couldn't count the number of times he'd longed for that conversation, for an explanation from his grandmother. Why did she leave so suddenly? Who would look after him? Jeremiah felt like a little child as these questions came up in his mind. Not going to her funeral left an eternal wondering about her leaving him. As he grew up, he understood, but a part of him still demanded answers.

Jeremiah recalled a dream he'd had that was eerily similar. His grandmother told him the same things as she did on the screen. *How did they know I needed this or that I'd thought and dreamt about this?*

Jeremiah didn't understand what was happening, but he was certainly grateful for it.

Suddenly, his tears were full of joy. The darkness in the room started to subside. Jeremiah didn't feel the overwhelming emptiness or darkness that had lived with him and had been portrayed perfectly by the room's eerie characteristics.

Jeremiah looked around the room again with clearer eyes. There was still not much in the room, but what was there was enough. He wrote a reply to his grandmother in his diary before leaving.

JOURNAL ENTRY, November 18, 2018

Dear Grandma,

Thank you so much for that moment I had with you in the "sadness room." It's never been the same here without you. But seeing you one more time, being your happy, joyful, loving self, has reaffirmed my strength in life.

I will put away those hurtful phrases Mum has said and keep the ones you used to tell me. How did I forget them?

I guess when you've been battered down so many times with negativity, and that's all you get, it's hard to see yourself differently. I will remember your kind words and laughter whenever I'm feeling down. I will remember this weird moment in this sad room and keep it present when I'm not feeling quite right.

I can do this, Grandma. I can do this. Watch me do it.

He felt young again, like before the anger, sadness, and bitterness took root. He grabbed hold of that feeling, picked up his journal, and headed to the bedroom for (hopefully) one last night. He was exhausted; it was a lot to take in.

Jeremiah was expecting to go into the third room the next day, but he would think about that after sleeping. He couldn't imagine it would be hard to fall asleep after all the stuff he'd just experienced in the second room.

He rested his head on the pillow and hoped he could dream with his grandma and continue that conversation.

CHAPTER 8

The Space Between

Jeremiah awoke the next morning feeling oddly refreshed. He realised he was still in that strange house. While he felt ready for the third room, he was wary about what he would encounter. What could he possibly have left to ponder on?

Let's think about it. The anger I'd been hanging on to had to do with stuff that happened when I was young, through my teenage years, which were particularly hard because Grandma died during those tricky times. I feel I was angry until very recently. Maybe I got better at working through the anger, or perhaps I just sent it to the back of my mind and body. Who knows?

Sadness; I'm more familiar with that, and it's definitely still with me—or is it after yesterday? I'll have to think more about that after breakfast. The question I had last night remains: will I still need alcohol like I did before coming to this house?

After rummaging through his thoughts for a little while longer, he stretched before soberly stepping out of bed. *That was much better than falling out like my first morning here.* Jeremiah confidently made his way to the kitchen for breakfast, not averting his eyes from the rooms upstairs.

Jeremiah felt replenished in mind and body after eating his favorite cereal for the third morning in a row. After retrieving his journal, he sat in front of the doors one final time. The two he'd already been in were full of sunlight—they weren't beckoning him anymore. He'd been there, done that. It was time to move on to the third door.

Wait a minute! Those two doors were about my past. What if this next one is about my present or even my future? But what could I possibly have to work on?

Jeremiah stood up with his journal in hand and opened the door with a confidence he'd lacked the previous two days. The room looked cheerful in the colour scheme. *Very Valentine's Day-ish,* he thought. He realised he was still standing at the threshold. After closing the door, he turned back to face the inside of the room. He noticed there were many figures dotted around the room, some standing really close to each other, while others were a bit more distant. In each pair, one figure was holding a card with his name on it.

Ah, so I have to read these cards, maybe? Let's see . . .

DISTANCE   FEAR   DESERVING   PERFECT LOVE

Jeremiah frowned, unsure of his purpose in this room. So, he lowered himself to the floor to sit and think, taking in the figures and how they were set up around the room. Flashbacks suddenly began after he allowed himself to fully accept the idea of these figures trying to communicate something to him. As in the "sadness room," he saw flashes of light behind the first couple of figures. What he saw made him half-smile and half-fill with regret and longing.

The half-smile was for the pleasant times he'd had with Lily. A smirk danced on his lips when he practically heard her say, "Don't call me that; call me Lils." *I could never do that, and I don't know why. Maybe if I did, it would mean we were getting serious?* Jeremiah's eyes focused on the word "Distance" held by the pair he was looking at when these thoughts entered his mind. *Is this about my relationship with Lily?*

The figure holding the card was very far away from its pair but was also looking away.

Jeremiah watched as a screen behind the pair stayed fixated on a particular scene, one he remembered clearly. He and Lily used to sit on a bench in the park near their houses—the same one every time. But with the emphasis placed on the word "distance," he realised they'd always sit on opposite ends of the bench—never touching, never looking at each other. But there was something powerful about their relationship— if he could call it that—in spite of it not being a traditional relationship.

A sense of desolation filled him for a moment. It was brief, but it showed him what he needed to see. He picked up his journal and wrote:

JOURNAL ENTRY, NOVEMBER 19, 2018

Lily was a big part of my life. But was she really? She was constantly physically there on that bench, at my home, at her house, at school . . . everywhere, but not much happened between us.

How can that be? How didn't I notice what was going on? Am I being too hard on myself here? If that worked for both of us, what's the problem?

But Jeremiah knew better. He knew the distance present in his relationship with Lily was a consequence of his relationship with his mother. He didn't understand how he came to this realisation. *What's up with these rooms? I've never thought about this in my life. Might as well go with it, or I might never leave this place.* He considered how he'd usually be grabbing a drink to deal with these questions. *Well, I would've been grabbing one about three days ago, to be honest.* It was a relief to him to not have that temptation. He knew that experiencing these rooms sober was helping him heal and not be dependent on alcohol.

Jeremiah sat for a little while, considering his thoughts. If he was looking at himself in a mirror, he'd be giving himself a suspecting, doubtful look, but at the same time, he was relieved not to be considering getting sloshed to make himself feel better. After a deep breath, he stood, shaking his head and bringing his consciousness back into the room as he moved to the second set of figures.

This pair were a bit closer together than the first, but the body language looked like they were fearful, almost pushing away from one another. Again, a flashback went through Jeremiah's mind while simultaneously displaying on the screen behind the figures. He was sharing a hug with his mum. From a distance, the embrace seemed genuine. But as the flashback panned to each of their facial expressions, Jeremiah could see his jaw was clenched, and his eyes were tightly shut. At the same time, his mum had an almost imperceptible but very present look of disgust arising from her lips and meeting in her eyes, which were looking at a distance, maybe somewhere she'd rather be than in that moment with her son.

The words, what are they? Ah! Fear and deserving. As he read them, he felt a twitch in his heart and a sinking feeling in his stomach. He sat there reading the words and glancing at the screen, which kept panning in and out of their faces, replaying the same scene over and over. *Disturbing.* He looked at the figures and realised they were fearful. But they also seemed doubtful. An urge came over him to grab his journal and write some more. This time it was longer.

JOURNAL ENTRY, November 19, 2018

Wow, this is hard. I thought the whirlwind in the angry room was bad. It wasn't as bad as the emptiness and darkness in the next room. Now, this! Glad there only seem to be three doors in this place, or I'd go mad. But will I be able to leave this place once this third nightmarish ordeal is over? Who knows?

Anyway, I'm doing what I always do. Deferring attention. Let's focus. Come on, Jeremiah, focus!

Ok. Fear. What are these figures afraid of? What was I afraid of when hugging Mum that day? Why am I crying again? Seriously, I'm going to run out of tears if this keeps up! Can't help it, though. I'm not a wimp for crying. Thanks, Mum! I'm going to cry if I need to and not fear any of the consequences of this. It is ok to cry, right? I think so. Well, tears are not stopping anyway, so not sure what telling me to man up would do. Blah blah blah. Can't hear you, Mum!

Yeah, that's the fear—the fact that I was never sure if she meant things. Was that hug genuine? It doesn't look like it from her scrunching up her face. Damn, it hurts to see that! I'm not going to look over there for a few minutes. Just look at the journal. Keep writing. It's safe in here. It always has been.

I was never scared sitting with Lily, even though not much happened. It was comfortable being with her in silence. We never touched or hugged, but we felt good together. It was as if we knew what we needed and didn't need to say anymore, or anything at all, really.

With Mum, it was like even when I shouted what I needed, I wasn't really heard. I never felt like I deserved anything. Deserving. That's the second word on there. I didn't feel like I deserved her love. She made me feel like I wasn't deserving of anything more than insults, shouts, and lots of ignoring.

Ha! I do deserve love. But now that I think about it, I'm terrified of it. Always have been except with Grandma, of course. She and I had a great relationship. We were so close; it really just worked. She never judged or questioned me. She just loved me the way I was.

Why did I only deserve Grandma's love? Why didn't I deserve my mother's love? Did Lily even love me, or was that just platonic or an ethereal relationship that was just what it was, no real meaning to fathom from it, but available at the right time, when I needed it the most?

Maybe that's how it happens? I have no idea. Didn't see it in my parent's relationship because my father was non-existent, and Mum never had anyone else. Grandma was on her own, a widow from the war, never remarried but spent her time giving to others. She was so lovely and special. Why did she have to die when I needed her the most?

Can't help thinking like that. She was the best. She was there for me like nobody else has been. Will I ever find that in anyone, ever? I don't know.

Reflecting on the impact Jeremiah's relationship with his mother had on him, he was somehow thankful for the flashback, for the memory of his time with Grandma and Lily, and even for the scrunching of his mum's face when hugging him. *Might as well have been hugging a slug or something with that face she made.* But he knew he wasn't a slug. He knew deep inside that he deserved love. He deserved what he'd experienced with Grandma and Lily.

Jeremiah realised there was one more set of figures he hadn't looked at yet. The words printed in the card they held together said, PERFECT LOVE. They were looking in each other's eyes, carefully holding the card in both of their hands, like a team. Like they were one.

This next flashback was a bit different. Almost prophetic. It was a flashback into the future—a flash-forward, perhaps. It also lasted a few minutes, unlike the other ones that were brief and seemed stuck in time. *Go figure, if they're about my past, then they kind of are, right?*

As he started watching, he thought how this flashback looked a lot like travel adverts, the ones where a beautiful lady is grabbing the unseen cameraman's hand, and she's showing him around beautiful places as the scenes change from location to location.

Jeremiah couldn't see the people's faces; they were either covered by hair or were looking in the opposite direction of where he was. All he saw was, at first, a beautiful brunette head of hair, flowing and swaying with the wind. She was setting up a picnic in a lovely garden near the sea. He could hear the waves. That's how he knew they were near the sea. She was carefully unfolding the blanket and placing some rocks to hold it down. She'd occasionally look up. He could hear her giggle. Suddenly, he realised she wasn't alone. Some children were playing in the distance, and a dog was following them. Again, he couldn't see their faces, only the dog's. The kids seemed to be having great fun, waving at the lady once in a while. Feeling safe in knowing that she was there, in case anything happened, they could run to her and be looked after. *Who are they? That's so nice that they can feel comfortable like that and smiling at what seems to be their mother. Who is she?*

The screen then played a rapid sequence of events: Jeremiah on his knee showing the lady with the picnic a ring; him in a tux waiting in a church; and him and someone wearing a white dress, walking out of the church. Finally, there was a hospital ward where he was staring at his first baby through the glass. *What is this? This hasn't happened? How can this be?*

He wrote in his journal for a final time.

JOURNAL ENTRY—FINAL FOR TODAY, November 19, 2018

Ok, this one is a shocker. But now that I think about it, Grandma told me a story once. I thought it was one of those stories, like Cinderella or something fictional like that. I never realised she'd been talking about what she hoped I'd have.

How am I figuring all this out? Was it always there, laid out for me by Grandma and the powers that be? Am I really deserving of the happiness I only knew with Grandma? Do I deserve the happiness I see in that scene of the future? My future?

If that's what perfect love looks like, God, I hope I'm worthy of it. I hope I live up to what that beautifully-haired lady expects of a husband. I wonder what Lily would think of her? I wonder what Grandma would think of her?

It's getting dark outside. I better get back to the bedroom and rest for a while. This has been highly draining. Third room's a charm! Hope tomorrow I wake up in my bed, with my own, current stuff. I would love to take you with me, my long-lost journal.

It's been quite a journey, which I'm not sure is over yet, but let's hope it is—as much as I've learned and re-lived. Not all pleasant, I must say. I don't want to do any more of this for now.

Good night.

JACOB

CHAPTER 9

Scaredy Cat

He had been sitting there, frozen. Jacob wasn't very good at "new things," and this one wasn't an average experience. He liked stability. Heck, he'd worked really hard to give himself a peaceful life, with things that made sense to him, that he loved and enjoyed.

This is weird. This isn't right. What are my transformers doing here? Lots of questions and thoughts were going through his head. Jacob practised his breathing exercises. They usually helped since his therapist suggested them. But this was beyond breathing in for four seconds, holding for two, and breathing out for four. He needed something more.

Jacob really wanted an explanation, but he couldn't hear anyone else in the house. He wasn't sure he was ready to leave the strange room yet to confirm his suspicions. *What if it's booby-trapped, and I get shot in the head as soon as I open the door?*

Jacob, he said to himself, *you're doing it again. You're letting your imagination get the best of you. I need Bill. He'd be able to help me figure this out. But he's not here. Nobody's here—I think.*

He continued trying to think rationally, to quench his rising adrenaline and cortisol levels, making him feel like fleeing —his usual response in challenging situations. But he didn't have anywhere to run, making him even more anxious.

Jacob, a self-confessed introvert, was working on making himself safe in situations that took him out of his comfort zone. But usually, these meant things like attending a party with people he barely knew or going to the shop to ask for his prescription. He'd practiced social situations with Bill so many times; he knew he could handle them. But there was nothing social about this. He was on his own with only his thoughts and feelings. Nobody was there to reassure him that this was all ok.

His insecurities got the best of him most of the time. *This is no time for insecurities. This is time for . . . for . . . Uhm. For something else.*

Survival?

Hang on, Jacob. Talking to himself helped. It was as if he was channelling Bill, his therapist for the past few years, and it calmed him down. He tried visualizing how he felt during his hardest sessions. *What exactly has happened that led you to think you might need to fight for your life here?*

Jacob continued his internal dialogue and found a way to ground himself by using techniques Bill had taught him. First, he looked at five things: transformers, his old thermos, an odd-shaped lamp in the corner, the dusty awful-looking mustard coloured curtains, the flowery wallpaper. *Eww, who decorated this room?* Next, he touched four things: the floor, his shoes, a fleece blanket, the door handle. *Wow, that felt odd.* Then, he listened for three things. *It's so quiet here, though. I can hear my heartbeat, the rustling of my clothes on the floor . . . we can hear silence, right?* Jacob inhaled hesitantly to smell two things. *I don't want to . . . Ah, that flower smells lovely. Lavender?* His nose crinkled at another scent. *My shoes need a good wash, that's for sure.* The final step was to taste one thing. He looked around at the various inedible objects, cringing at the thought of licking the wallpaper when he eyed a candy bar. *Is that Snickers bar old, or can I eat it? What the heck? Let's give it a go.*

As he took a bite of the candy bar, Jacob closed his eyes for a brief moment, hoping to open them to his usual familiar surroundings. To his dismay, he saw the same things he'd been focusing on a few moments prior. He couldn't find his phone or a clock, but he assumed it had to be around mid-morning. *I'm going to have to go out into the rest of the house at some point. Geez, I hate new things and situations.*

Jacob's dislike of things out of the ordinary had been a focus of many of his sessions. None of what he learned, though, would save him from being in that strange house. He pondered on his predicament and weighed his options. The odds weren't good. In fact, the odds seemed to be quite against him.

Jacob stood up slowly, still taking in what he saw around the room he mysteriously woke up in. He gathered he needed to go to the door. When he touched the door handle, a gush of emotions overcame him. He immediately let go of it. All he could do was think about all the times he'd sat in his room or his therapist's office, overwhelmed, unable to move or shift or do much but cry and hit a pillow.

He shook his head to try to shake the memories away. It helped some, but they were still there, haunting him like old ghosts who had become odd friends—familiar beings in his life. It felt like a continuous presence reminding him of things he'd rather forget. *I really need to see what's out there. Come on, Jacob. Open the flippin' door!*

He was frozen with fear to the spot. Jacob's eyes darted around the room again. He hadn't even opened the mustard curtains to see where he was. That was how extensive his discomfort was. *Unease is more like it. Terror? Ok, maybe that's taking it a bit far.*

Catastrophising, Bill had told him, was Jacob's middle name in times of uncertainty. He'd made peace with the fact that this is who he was. It didn't mean he liked it but befriending rather than fighting had been a good strategy he'd been working on with Bill.

Jacob spent another five minutes contemplating the dusty door handle. He could almost feel the cortisol running through his veins. *Get a grip, Jacob! No, literally, grip that handle and open it.*

As he opened the door, Jacob felt an unwelcome adrenaline rush. He could almost hear his inner self scream. He was at the top of a huge landing looking out to a huge space with high ceilings, and a spiral staircase, like something out of *Titanic*. The banisters looked ancient but eerily beautiful. He felt the urge like he'd had when he was younger to slide down them. *Maybe later. Maybe when I feel more comfortable in this God-forsaken place.*

Dramatic much? Well, you know me. I like drama—internal drama, but drama nonetheless.

Looking, eyes wide open, Jacob noticed three doors that stood out from the rest. He felt drawn to them, curious, but something about them terrified him. The pull towards them was enough for him to forget himself and his usual caution.

Jacob's feet seemed to move of their own accord, but he stopped a few feet in front of the door, overwhelmed with emotion. His analytical mind couldn't make sense of what was happening. *Nobody can make sense of whatever this is.* Jacob decided to go back to the room he awoke in. He needed to gather himself and his thoughts and do some more breathing.

He felt his chest heaving as soon as he reentered the familiar-strange place. Up and down, Jacob took in more air to calm himself.

Jacob's ability to focus on something other than what was happening helped him to ground himself. He grabbed ahold of the curtains. *These are awful! I'm gonna have a talk with the decorator when I get out of here—the colour, the pattern . . . Geez! Who lives like this?*

He pulled open one of the curtain panels and was astounded by what he saw. It was beautiful: freshly cut grass and beautiful flowers of all kinds, some he'd never seen before. Someone had put a lot of care and time into this. He wanted to go outside and smell each one of them, take in the whole thing. *Whoever put me here must've known I enjoy flowers and feel safe around them. It reminds me of a better time, before the catastrophe.* It had taken Bill and Jacob months for him to put words into his way of being in the world. Survival mode was what they'd labelled it. Through some trial and error, they discovered looking at pretty flowers was something that helped overcome the overwhelming sensations.

"Bill, is this your idea?" Jacob looked around the room for cameras. He felt that this was highly unethical for a therapist to place a patient in such a cruel, bizarre situation. *I must be dreaming. This can't be real.* He paced in front of the window, shifting his gaze between the outside and inside. Finally, he touched the curtains again. *But everything I've touched feels real. What's happening?*

His stomach grumbled, causing him to groan. Jacob didn't want to leave the room, but aside from the old candy bar he already ate, there was nothing. He was unsure of whether there'd be food, but surely whoever put him there wouldn't want him to starve to death.

Jacob made his way downstairs, quietly, carefully, watching and listening for anything that could signal danger. Nothing happened—nothing except finding the food his body was asking him to ingest. He ate and drank in his usual pensive manner. His meal times, similarly to his shower times, were his best "thinking times." He got lost in his thoughts— *a way to set the world right, even if just for a moment.* Satiated, he felt in a better frame of mind to consider his options.

In his mind, Jacob felt he had four options: *leave this house and find a way to get back home; stay and explore because maybe I'm locked in here; fall asleep and hope I wake up in my own bed next time; hide, but from who, there hasn't been a sign of life since I woke up.*

He decided to check the front door—a huge wooden slat, it looked thick and very sturdy—to see if the option to escape was plausible. Jacob turned the handle, but it didn't budge, and there was no key in sight. *Ok, option B it is, or maybe C. Being asleep might be better than wandering around someone else's house. Whose house is this anyway?* Another question with no answer. He was getting used to that. No answers. Just questions.

●　●　●

Belly full, body calmer, he pulled a chair near the window in his new room and lost himself in thought. Jacob looked at the beauty that was before him—albeit outside and out of reach. But still, it was very beautiful. It gave him peace and space to think and prepare himself to face whatever was next.

Gathering his strength, Jacob got up from his daydreaming near the window. Walking around the house, getting a glimpse of what his new reality was—locked in this castle-like place, with unusual rooms that gave him strange but familiar reactions.

As he walked around, he glanced at the front door again and thought about the things he'd encountered so far. *Locked in. Trapped. My old prized possessions. The lovely garden outside. Me and my memories. My thoughts. My feelings.*

Am I meant to do something with all of this? What can I do? Jacob decided to return to his room and sit by the window for a bit longer and enjoy the view. There didn't seem to be a hurry there. He wouldn't know, anyway, if he was late or early or right on time—there were no clocks or any way to communicate with the outside world.

Jacob reflected on something his therapist told him repeatedly: *"Be in the moment, Jacob." Is that why I'm here? To learn to be in the moment more? This seems like a strange and extreme way of learning how to do that.*

CHAPTER 10

The Intruders

"Intruders" was the name he and Bill had named the thoughts that came out of nowhere. Jacob could already feel "them" crowding around, awaiting their turn. These intruders were disparaging, evil, rude, mean, insulting, and last but not least, frightening. *Yay, my favourite, frightening! Like I'm not frightened enough by just going to the shop to get a single item. Just what I need, the intruders to come along.* Jacob planned to say that to Bill in one of their future sessions.

As a self-confessed-and-happy-to-proclaim-it introvert, Jacob usually kept to himself wherever he went. He could care less about small talk, or so he told himself. *Maybe I can't think of anything to talk about?* "Be more honest," Bill had told him. "If you're honest with yourself, others will accept that this is you, but if you don't, then they won't either."

Jacob continued to explore the house. Everything was very dramatic—large pieces of furniture and huge sculptures staring at him at every corner. He wasn't scared of them, but he thought they were strange indeed. Looking around, he focused again on the ginormous staircase where he'd gone down to get some food. His attention being drawn insistently toward the beckoning rooms. They looked eerily unassuming like they were avoiding his glance. As he left his thoughts about what his therapist had said, he felt drawn to one of the rooms on the opposite side of the hall.

Jacob decided it was time to face whatever was behind "door number one!" (said in that presenter's voice from the eighties, *Supermarket Sweep*, no the other one, *The Price is Right.*). *Is this really a time to joke around like that, Jacob? When things are looking a bit serious, you decide to make a joke?*

YOU CAN'T DO THIS.

And there it was. Jacob knew the intruder would come. At least it was just one, for now.

YOU CAN'T DO THIS.

"I can, and I will. Just watch me!" As Jacob said these words, he approached the god-forsaken door that kept luring him toward it. When he got closer, he noticed the floor was different. It still had an awful flower pattern, but it became less ugly and less, well, flat. The ground was suddenly looking a lot like the garden outside; small, beautiful flowers, following the carpet's original pattern, but in 3D, were flowering in front of his eyes. They were bright and beautiful to his eyes; he could almost smell them too. He was a few feet away from them when he noticed he noticed they were withering just as quickly as they'd blossomed. *Oh, doom!* he thought. This was one of the phrases he was working on eradicating. Still, given the circumstances, he thought them very appropriate and refused to come up with a milder or less "catastrophic" alternative.

The thought of the intruder telling me one more time, "I can't do this," is making me squirm and wanna puke. When Jacob finally opened the door, he stood there, frozen for what felt like an eternity. He was amazed and scared all at once. There were flowers of all kinds covering the entire room—even the furniture had flowers growing out of it. *What IS this place?* He couldn't understand what was happening to him, much less yet where he was, but the magic he was encountering enthralled him. *There's no other word or explanation for this; it must be magic.*

As soon as Jacob had that thought, the door slammed shut behind him. He realised he'd taken slow steps into the room. Mesmerised by the view, he'd forgotten caution for a moment and instantly regretted it. He ran to the door and tried to open it, but couldn't. With his back turned away from the room, he felt a chill running down the spine, and he immediately knew what was behind him. *The intruders! It can't be.* He froze, not wanting to move. *Maybe they won't see me. Maybe if I stay still, the door will unlock, and I can be free of this.*

Of course, that didn't happen.

As he gathered the courage, he recalled Bill's words from the last hundred sessions and took deep breaths—four seconds in, hold for two, four seconds out. Finally, he turned around to face whatever fate would befall him. Thunder-like flashes were the first thing he saw, followed by unrecognisable speaking. He fell to his knees and covered his ears. The next bit of thunder hit him like a ton of bricks. The voice was unmistakable:

YOU CAN'T DO THIS.

Again, like he'd heard before entering the room, and like so many times before. That time, he'd heard it in his mind, in his voice. In the room, it was outside of him. *In the form of thunder? How can something inside of me also be outside of me?* Even in Jacob's thoughts, that didn't make sense. *Am I going crazy? Am I imagining things? What is going on? Can I just have the earth swallow me and take me back to my bed?*

But he knew that wasn't going to happen. There was something about the place he'd woken up in that was telling him he had to be there, *in that moment*, like Bill liked to repeat to him on and off. *Ok, I can do this. What proof do I have that I can do this? I've never done this before.* He picked up one of the flowers in front of him, and on one of its petals, it said:

YOU CAN DO THIS.

As soon as Jacob read it, the thunder came again, followed by lightning hitting the flower in his hands, turning it into ash, which seeped through his hands and fell to the floor. He froze again, staring with wide eyes at his hands. While unscorched, he was shaking from the commotion left after the destruction of the beautiful flower.

"I can do this!" he shouted in the middle of the room. He cried and repeated it many times over. *I can do this. I can do this. I can do this.* The intruders were powerful, but they only had as much power as Jacob allowed them to have. Somehow, he had to fight the thunder and keep it from destroying the flowers. *But how?* He knew more intruders would eventually show up—it was only a matter of time. What was it he'd heard over and over and over again? *Your voice is your super-power, Jacob. Use it well.*

The last time he used it well, it backfired on him. He was laughed at and ridiculed. Maybe he'd done it wrong? Maybe he needed more practice? *Well, too late for that,* he thought, looking at all the flowers and ash around him. He dreaded the thought of more of the beautiful flowers being destroyed. He continued to admire the beautiful colours and variety of flowers in the room, hoping that it would stay this quiet forever. It had just been a few minutes since the last intruder "attacked." Suddenly, Jacob felt pangs in his belly, which signalled the next wave coming. He was an avid gamer, and in some of his games, waves of zombies took over the land. There was always a telling sign that they were about to appear and wreak havoc everywhere. He always had pangs of excitement when that moment happened. In that room, though, it was mostly dread.

He likened his intruders to the zombies he'd killed many times in his gaming adventures. He braced himself for what was coming, preparing his weapon—his voice—hoping for the best. Before the wave began, he noticed the flowers were speaking to him. He could hear them reciting the counter-arguments to the intruders like he'd practiced so many times throughout the previous years. *How is this happening? I don't understand. Are these flowers my weapons? But they're getting obliterated by the thunder. Ok, ok, let me grab a few and get ready for the intruders then. Let's see what happens. Geez, this is weird, but somehow I'm still standing and not completely frozen. That's a change.*

YOU CAN'T DO THIS.

As he saw these words for the millionth time, it seemed. Jacob diverted his eyes down at one of the flowers he'd picked up. It was telling him of a time where he could and did do something. He remembered his brother teasing him that he couldn't go across the big-kid monkey bars on his own. He was almost in tears; the mocking was so bad. He had, after all, fallen flat on his face a few times prior. But he wasn't to be defeated. His dad was nearby, watching what was happening. In his support for Jacob, he told his brother to step away and be quiet. *Dad then came over to me, put his hands around my legs, supporting me, and telling me that I could do it, that he wouldn't let go until I was ready.* So, Jacob began crossing the monkey bars, reaching one bar after the next, gaining confidence as he did. With five more to go, he told his dad to let go, and he made it across without wavering.

Jacob smiled and thought how lucky he was to have such an understanding and caring dad. His brother, on the other hand, had some growing up to do back then. As he smiled, he felt another wave of thunder and lightning strike coming, but this time the flower caught it, and it dissipated as quickly as it appeared. After just a few moments of respite, another blast happened, tearing through the room like a thousand watery shouts.

YOU'RE USELESS!

The next set of words cut him deeply. He fell to his knees, trying to shield his eyes from them, but it was almost impossible. There were piles of ash—once beautiful flowers—in front of him and one flower sitting on top. It almost felt like it was staring at him, urging him to pick it up. *Ah, the intruder solution. Let's see what it says, or does, for that matter. All of this is very strange but oddly therapeutic. Too bad Bill isn't here to see this or hear me say this. Maybe I'll fill him in later, whenever I get out of here.*

As he picked up the flower, he felt overwhelming helplessness, along with a sense of unfairness. He needed there to be justice. *But about what?* He couldn't think. He went blank. Suddenly, another set of thunder and lightning hit a few flowers next to him. He looked and knew a second intruder had joined—these specific two usually attacked in pairs.

LOOK AT YOU. CAN'T EVEN MOVE, CAN YOU?

Jacob froze. *Oh no, not the paralysis. I don't think I can do much right now.* As he thought that, the flower began to glow softly. It was just enough for him to shift his focus from feeling useless and notice the words written on its petals:

YOUR JOURNEY, YOUR TERMS,
MOVE AT YOUR PACE.

As soon as Jacob read that, he went back into his memories again. He sat down as he went deep in thought. This time, he went to a time where he felt he had to follow his dad's life path in order to be useful or to prove that he could do this thing called life. He was sitting on his bed, crying with frustration. He must have been crying so hard and audible enough for his father to come in and check on him. His dad was always very supportive of him. His approval didn't depend on what he did or didn't do—it was just about who he was. Jacob was his son, and that's all that mattered. That was one reason why it was so important for him to be like his dad—caring and understanding, but also stern, serious, boundaried, self-sufficient, capable, professional, and successful in most of what he put his mind to as an entrepreneur.

Jacob wanted to be just like his dad, but that was proving very difficult, as he forced himself to do things he thought were the right thing for himself. That evening, his dad asked him what the matter was. Jacob told him about his struggles with his current business attempts—he was only eighteen but had lots of dreams he wanted to achieve sooner than later.

Jacob told his dad that he wanted to be more courageous, more outspoken, more of a leader than a follower. He wanted to learn how to be like him. His dad smiled big and gave him a big squishy hug, only like he could do. He ended the embrace by ruffling Jacob's hair a bit as he had lovingly done all of Jacob's life.

They talked for what seemed to be a long, long time, but Jacob only remembered the words written on the petals of this pretty flower he was holding on to fiercely: *your journey, your terms, move at your own pace.*

HA HA HA HA HA!

The last usual suspect, the fourth intruder, showed up. This one seemed like the lesser of the four evils, but it disturbed and unsettled Jacob even more than the other ones. It wasn't explicit in its attack. It just laughed in this mocking, evil way that made him shiver and retreat every time it showed its ugly face—or sound, in this case.

Jacob had worked on this intruder for a long time. He'd managed to make it such a small-sounding thing that he could carry on, even if it persevered on mocking him from the corners of his mind. What he did next surprised even him. Jacob stood up with one move, something he wouldn't have thought he could do. *You can't do this,* the first intruder croaked at him from its ashy grave on the floor. It turned out the thunder and lightning that carried it hadn't dissipated completely; its leftovers were joined by its initial flower victim. *Is that what happens to me every time these intruders succeed? A bit of me dies? Geez, I hope not. I'm not going to put up with this any longer, but I'm not sure what to do. What can I do? Is any of it under my control? Where do these intruders come from? How do I shut them up?*

As Jacob was thinking all of this, getting himself into a tizzy, he sat down in the corner of the room, looking at all the mess the thunderous intruders created. He felt a surge of strength come from deep within him, and when he spoke, the flowers blossomed again. The words he said were inconsequential. He noticed the effect his voice had on the flowers and realised it had been there within him all along. He opened up his mouth again, shouted, *"Aaaahhh!"* and watched in amazement as the flowers engulfed the origin of the thunder and lightning bolts—the source of the intruders. These were the thoughts that constantly plagued and unsettled him no end.

That felt good. Like in Jacob's game when he'd decimated the last wave of zombies by himself with his team. In the aftermath, they could stop holding their breath and vivaciously pressing the controller buttons and just walk around the land and survey the damage. They could pick up health and recover their lost items, which they'd use in another attack in a few days. Right now, it was time to rebuild. *Hmm, time to rebuild. On my own terms this time, maybe? Maybe there's a way to be like my father but do it my way, as well—a way that makes sense to me, not something prescribed for someone else that worked for them.* He pondered on this for a while, sitting near the window where he could see another angle of the garden. He repeated the empowering phrase over and over, gaining strength at each repetition.

My journey. I will move at my pace.

• • •

As those last thoughts entered his mind, Jacob felt exhausted. Everything was happening so fast. He stood up, resolutely—something he'd never done before. Usually, he would've remained in the corner for hours until it was unreasonable to stay put, and the imminent dangers had seemed to pass. *There's no real lion. You're not in the jungle. Fight or flight or freeze isn't necessary here.* He understood those words from Bill even more now. Loud and clear. In fact, he knew he could do this; Jacob knew he wasn't useless, that he could move—darn it, he was moving.—and the internal mocking wasn't going to stop him any longer.

Jacob smiled when he turned the knob and walked out of the room. *I must've achieved this room's purpose then, right? What does that mean?* He tried not to overthink it but remembered his therapist saying something about having to do a personal development group during his counselling course and to this day, nobody knew what it had done for each of them, but that it had done something. *Sounds strange, but Bill's training doesn't sound like it was easy. He did say they all were walking around raw—like I feel right now. It makes more sense now, in hindsight.*

Jacob changed into his pyjamas and settled into bed. *Tomorrow will be another day, another room. I'll think about it tomorrow, in good Scarlett O'Hara fashion.*

CHAPTER 11

No Man Is an Island

Jacob remained lying in bed after waking up. He'd always been like that—lethargic at the start of the day. It usually took him a few snoozes on his phone's alarm to finally be awake enough to get up. He felt slightly different waking up that following morning—full of energy and empowered from the previous day's happenings.

He spent some time meditating in bed on why such delicate flowers were magically growing all over that room, giving him hints and tools to get himself up and moving to challenge the intruders. *"Intrusive thoughts" are only as powerful as you let them be*, Bill once told him; he was always full of psychobabble gems that surprisingly worked for Jacob.

He felt like he might be like those flower petals. But also, Jacob loved flowers. The thoughts carried him from the bed to sit by the window and gaze at the flowers in the garden. He craved to be able to smell, touch, and just be around those beautiful creations. *Who created it? Who took the time to make that garden so beautiful like that?*

Jacob had never been religious. Even that word made him cringe. He got that from his mum, who cringed at the word, stating over and over that she wasn't religious; she had a relationship with Christ. His mum had minimal impact on his life, except for that. He wasn't sure yet whether he was thankful for it or not. But just thinking about creation and how it couldn't have been random, he remembered his mum's words about Jesus: "*He loves you no matter what. He suffered for all of our sins, died, and rose again so we could live life more abundantly. All you have to do is let him into your heart and read His word regularly, and He will speak to you and give you what you need.*" That was all he remembered. He was lucky he didn't get the Bible-bashers on him, or it would've warped that lovely memory of his mum speaking those words to him and dismissed in his mind, tucked away with the other repressed and forgotten things he found either traumatic or irrelevant. He had never known what to do with "the God thing," but he kept it close to his heart—just in case.

Jacob resolved to get out of bed and start the adventure in the next room. *Who knows what wildflowers might be growing in there. Ha! Have I figured it out? Now that I'm not stuck to the spot, thanks to last night, I feel braver to explore, but still, the cautious way of being is there, trying to hold me back. I guess I'll go back and forth with this until it settles. Like Bill always says, "It's a process, Jacob; give it time, and be kind to yourself."*

There was something about Bill and their relationship that led Jacob to stay with him longer than his other therapists. Those others didn't "get him" in the way that Bill did. He understood. He listened. He was patient. They just gelled. Jacob felt safe in Bill's office, and even when they had online sessions, he could forget that he was in his bedroom. It seemed like he was transported to a safe space with Bill, where he could open up and be himself in spite of everything overwhelming he'd felt through the last few years. Throughout all the angry words, curse words, crying, shouting, and hair-pulling, Bill had been a constant, calming presence. Jacob was channelling that while he worked through whatever he was meant to do in this house, wherever, whenever, and however it was.

Jacob didn't have many friends, which troubled him somewhat because everyone else seemed to have great big parties, reunions, or events. He did have a handful of trusted friends that he could talk to—like two or three, but still. They were top-notch. Mostly, he was a loner.

As Jacob thought that last thought, he got up from the seat by the window, put his clothes on, and walked towards the doors. He wasn't big on breakfast, but he hadn't had much since he mysteriously arrived at that house. He tended to skip meals when he was worried or overwhelmed—*some people are overeaters; I'm an under-eater.* He couldn't eat or think of food when his mind was full of everything else. This was where mind met body. His body was his thermometer for when he was feeling strong emotions, was distressed, worried, or unhappy. *Maybe that's why the flowers were there: physical beings that mirrored me, who I've been, how I've felt.* It seemed the words on the petals that encouraged him were also deep within him, but he hadn't used those resources before. He'd read about that in a book about boundaries or something like that. It hadn't clicked then, but Bill always said, "Let things simmer for a bit, and then when the time is right, you'll get there and start putting the things we discussed or read about into practice." *How is that man always right? I guess he's been doing this for a while now. I trust him and his methods work; that's all that matters.*

• • •

As Jacob approached the second door, he suddenly had a thought about the flowers and quickly ran back to the bedroom to look out the window. The whole garden had turned an odd, yellow tone, glowing in spite of the sun shining strongly on them. *Hmm, that's not how that was yesterday. I would remember a yellow-only garden! What is happening in this place?* As he was saying that, the flowers seemed to flicker and slowly change into a bland beige—still glowing but beige. He wondered what he was about to encounter, deep in thought as he considered making his way back to today's beckoning door. He was trying to fight the fear, but it was still too soon for his newly found courage to become his new way of being.

Jacob knew that shade of beige. He used to spend hours on his paint-by-numbers as a child and even as a teenager. It was how he avoided social situations like the plague. He enjoyed his own company. *Or did I convince myself I enjoyed being alone rather than feeling lonely on my own? It felt like a good compromise, I guess.* One of the most common colours he painted with was beige. It was easy to change it to something else by adding a layer of another colour, but it also allowed him to emphasise other parts of the painting. *Emphasis, huh. Oh, God! What am I going to be paying attention to in this flippin' room? I really don't want to do this right now. But do I have a choice? Geez, why is this so hard? They are harmless rooms. They are harmless. They are harmless. They are . . .*

Jacob was startled mid-sentence by a loud thump from the doors outside his room. He walked over to the door, and as stealthily as he could—just like he'd done so many times whilst playing *Tomb Raider*—he looked from behind the bedroom door and noticed a similar beige hue seeping out of the room, like a surreal cloud, luring him into the second door.

He gathered himself with his usual calming techniques, and with his newly found lack of "freezing-ness," as he called it, he confidently marched over to the room, opened the door, and found himself staring at two things. The first one was a large flowerpot with what looked like a sunflower, but he wasn't quite sure if it was that. The second one was a large painter's table, set at an angle for ease when painting, a palette with some colours on it, and a paint-by-number looking drawing on the table.

Jacob's mind went everywhere. He stood there for a few seconds—in typical Jacob fashion. Only twelve hours prior—and even earlier that morning—he felt he'd overcome the instinct to freeze. Perplexed, Jacob realised the change in behavior couldn't work that fast. He accepted that: *acceptance, another one of Bill's favourite words.*

Once Jacob felt able to move again, he slowly and carefully walked towards the flower; he was always afraid that a sudden, abrupt noise would scare him half to death and send him into the corner, a frozen, unfocused, and unrelenting mess. Nothing happened. *Phew.* The flower started glowing again, changing to different blue, brown, grey, and black hues.

Oddly enough, as Jacob turned to look at the table and palette set up for him, those same colours were waiting for him to delve in. He had been so focused on the flower that he hadn't paid much attention to the drawing. Again, very slowly, he approached it. He didn't want to shock the system.

As he got closer, Jacob noticed the painting wasn't just one big painting; it was more like a comic strip, like those old-fashioned comic books that had short stories but made their point very well. Each page of these books had at least three shorts that told a whole story.

He prepared the colours and brushes. A water cup for cleaning the brushes was also sitting there. He quickly realised he was meant to colour the pictures in. *This will be fun. I haven't painted in a while, but I'm sure this is part of the experience. Bill always said that having a hobby that made sense to me, apart from the gaming stuff, would be good for me, especially when times got tough.*

Short One

The first box was a bit inconsequential. It showed a young-looking lad staring at a screen while holding a wireless game controller. There was a speech box that read, "Joe, why aren't you killing them? Come on, man. Get moving!" Jacob remembered that. It was him in the drawing, playing video games with his friends from all over the world. He wasn't skilled at being social with people near him, but with voices on the games, easy peasy.

The next box made him cringe a bit. The drawing was of him smashing his controller. That day had been awful for him. After a long stint of playing online, paying his membership so he could talk to his online gamer friends, his computer died. He couldn't afford to buy a new one. He was all alone, even more, without access to the one thing that kept him company—the group of people he knew but didn't really know, but somehow it still worked.

The third box made him shed a tear as he recalled how he felt. It revealed Jacob cowered in the corner of his room, holding the pieces of what once was so dear to him. In one fell swoop, he'd destroyed his only link to sanity that he had. Asking for help wasn't his forte, and asking his mum or dad for some money to buy a new computer wasn't an option at that point. With his new mindset, he would've asked them to lend him some money with less hesitation, although still doubting the importance of his request. Would they get it? Would they understand? Did he need to explain why this was so important to him? He'd promise to pay them back as soon as he could. If there was something reliable about Jacob, it was his word.

By the time he'd worked through the three boxes in the first short, the scenes were coloured. He'd managed to make the colours less lonely looking by mixing them and making new colours. He was creative that way, even though he'd never give himself credit for it.

Throughout this painting session, Jacob felt a deep hole growing inside of him, the kind that always made him lose his appetite. No, it wasn't the feeling of being alone. It was loneliness—the familiar feeling of loneliness. He didn't feel a part of this world even though he was right in the middle of it. Sometimes, he loved being an introvert and a loner, but when things got hard—like the computer dying and leaving him in despair—he loathed the fact that there was hardly anyone he could reach out to. Bill was there, of course, but that wasn't the same. He was reassuring and helpful and had gone through a lot with Jacob, but he wasn't a friend. It was a professional "therapeutic relationship," as Bill had called it on their first session. Even so, it had become an essential part of his life.

Jacob was craving, in real-time, what he had craved for so many times in the past: a group of people to laugh with, to watch movies with, to just sit and stare at the sea or garden, or to travel with and explore new things. *How do people do this? How do people get friends and keep them? Maybe it's going to happen for me. But what do I need to do?*

Short Two

As if in answer to his question, the second short appeared. How did that just happen? It had only one large box in it. As ever, Jacob's mind was reeling with questions mixed with fear, disconcert, and some expectation, which was a new one for him. He noticed a change in light, and as he turned, he saw the flower had become bright blue. He looked back at the palette and chose the bright blue colour for this next vignette.

The only box in this short showed someone that looked like Jacob but wearing old-fashioned garb, like from the 1940s: checkered jacket, which was blueish-green by the time he finished colouring it, and a Gatsby style hat. Under the jacket, there was a well-ironed white shirt with brown suspenders attached to the dark brown trousers—an average gentleman's cut—to match the jacket and suspenders. He looked very dapper. Why is there so much detail on this dude? Who is he? Jacob quickly realised it wasn't about who this guy was; it was more about what he was doing.

This same scene showed the guy's silhouette moving across the long space, carrying out various activities. On one, he was talking on the phone, and the speech bubble read, "Great! See you then." The next one showed him writing on a pad, which said, "Jane's surprise birthday plans." Who's Jane? This dude's girlfriend or wife? The next couple of moving silhouettes showed the guy arranging furniture while some party decorations were visible in the background.

Jacob was a bit confused by this short, which he continued to ponder as he coloured it in. He noticed that the palette didn't have just those sad, lonely colours anymore. It had added some yellows, purples, and other fun shades. Jacob painted with interest in the different silhouettes of the same man, being very active in pursuing social activities.

Then it clicked—the picture reminded him of a conversation he'd had with an online friend. They didn't know much about each other; maybe that's why it worked so well. In spite of very little personal details, they could go into great detail about their current struggles. *Those who say that social media or gaming causes mental health should come into my head and see how much it has actually helped me stay sane. That time without my computer was almost deadly. I didn't harm myself, probably 'cause I'm a bit of a scaredy-cat, but still, it could've gone either way. The loneliness was certainly real. It was awful, but it's passed. I've got my new computer, and it works great. I can't spend that much time gaming anymore because I have to work, but it's still great to go to those guys online and have a good chat and some laughs.*

His online friend had said to him that he wasn't that social either. But he was fine with that—people were weird anyway. All that small talk trying to fit in wasn't for him. To pretend to smile at someone when you were about to die with shame, embarrassment, or just sheer boredom—as the topics of conversation were mostly beneath him—was torture. Of course, Jacob wasn't as extreme as his friend, but he got the idea. Socialising isn't for everyone. Everyone has to find their own way of doing things. Bill had hinted at that, as well, but dropped it when Jacob started to get upset. Bill knew when to pick things up and when to let them go. He'd told Jacob many times: *This is you, we don't need to talk about this now, it will come back at a later time when you're more ready.* Jacob was glad he didn't have to face things he wasn't ready to face—dealing with his socialising issues had been one of the bigger issues, and he was glad it was taken slowly and at his pace.

As Jacob finished painting the vignette, he started feeling expectant, hopeful that he'd not always feel lonely as he had in the past. He felt the loneliness even in that room, calm as it was, with the weird colour-changing flower in there and the palette guiding him by changing colours as well. He didn't fully understand what was happening, but he wasn't as afraid as he was the first day. Maybe he was gathering strength to make friends too? To trust others to like and know him, warts and all. *Maybe, just maybe, people won't mind the things I like to talk about. Maybe they'll even laugh at my unsavoury jokes. I don't know. It's worth a shot, right?*

Short Three

Jacob approached the last short with a smile. He felt much less lonely and could see himself more involved with his family and even with some friends. The three vignettes showed a smiling young lad. In the first one, he was hugging his apparent girl-friend, who appeared to like him a lot. Wow, she's a hottie and way out of his league. But hey, she chose to be there. He might as well accept that he had something to do with it. He must be likeable for more than just physical looks. I mean, he's not ugly, but compared to her, he's just average. Maybe those things don't matter as much? I wonder when I'll get a girlfriend. Will she be as pretty? What will she like about me? Will she tell me?

The second scene showed a bunch of people laughing and having fun, including the young man from the first scene. As he coloured this one in, he felt excited to be able to do something like this. But maybe not as many people; a handful would be fine. He wanted to go out and find these people, make plans, and enjoy their company. He wasn't sure if this feeling would last—always the doubter—but he was enjoying the experience nonetheless.

The final scene showed the young man lying in bed, arms above his head, in a relaxed pose, with a smile on his face.

Well, it seems like this lad has everything he needs. There's hope for me yet.

CHAPTER 12

Words Unspoken

Jacob enjoyed the comic strips with what eerily resembled his life, past, present, and possible future. *Possible future? How could these people, whoever they are, know about this? It's all in my head.* He didn't realise that this thought was exactly what was happening to him in that house. His deepest, darkest, most repressed feelings, thoughts, and fears were being manifested in the rooms, just as he felt them every day of his life, but in a more visible, tangible way. Was he really in this place? Was he dreaming? Was this something like what happened in that book his mum loved to read, *The Shack*, where a guy who lost his kid went to the shack where she died and met God in an interesting and surreal way? But that character had driven his car to that place; he had consciously taken himself there, and was fully aware of what he was doing, who he was, where he was going. *Will I ever find out? All I know is that this feels very real, although some of it is very surreal. Wait 'til I tell Bill! Should I? He might get in touch with his psychiatrist friend and have me committed for the rest of my life!*

As Jacob got out of bed after his morning musings, he went to the window to check out the garden. It was back to normal—well, the normal he'd experienced when he first saw it. He wondered what the last room would bring him. The other two had been very scary, interesting, enlightening, and even frustrating. He was amazed at what seeped out of the flowers, the comic strips, and even the colours. *Powerful stuff,* he thought as he made his way from the bedroom to the kitchen, grabbed a piece of toast with butter, and walked over to the rooms. The third one beckoned him, but he wasn't sure what he'd find yet on the other side of the door.

Without much further hesitation, he swung the door open.

The flower theme continued, covering the carpet and the walls, but they were just there as reminders. They didn't seem to do anything or have any writing on their petals. Jacob still smiled at their sight. They'd given him interesting experiences in the other rooms. Why wouldn't they be in this third room?

Suddenly, a new kind of intruder Jacob wasn't expecting dashed across his line of sight. A flash of light, not unlike the lightning, but not as fierce or worthy of Jacob's furious fear. He chased it around the room like you would a firefly you wanted to use as a lantern while camping. He was familiar with that, as he'd done it so many times during camping trips with his family. To avoid his brother's bullying, he'd lose himself in the woods, leaving without telling anyone but his dad so he wouldn't worry and so he would deter the other ones from going to look for him.

After what felt like an eternity, Jacob caught the light. It was very fidgety in his hands, so he waited until it calmed and stopped moving. As he waited, he felt the unidentified object change in his hands. It seemed to be transforming into something else. He opened his hands, and as he did so, a letter unfolded in front of him. It fell like a leaf falls from a tree, swaying back and forth in the wind, flowing with it, but being pushed slowly down by gravity until it landed on the flower-patterned carpet.

Jacob was unsure how it happened, though it jogged a memory of a magician's trick he'd seen when he was younger. The magician had taken a twenty-pound note from a punter, and he'd folded it very tightly—so tightly that it became tiny.

It was so small it was hardly noticeable when he performed his disappearing act, leaving the punter twenty pounds poorer, but pleased with what he'd just witnessed. *Maybe that's what's happened here but in reverse?* He didn't know how that had ended or if the guy ever got his twenty bob back. He'd giggled at the magician asking someone for "twenty bob" in an accent that was far from cockney. It had made his day!

As Jacob recalled the magician, he picked up the letter and sat down on a surprisingly comfortable chair camouflaged by the flowery patterns. The letter wasn't very long, but it was enough for him to realise that they were his own words. They were words he'd ever expressed to anyone but would have loved to have done. More than a letter, it included phrases he'd wanted to say to people, all bundled into one sheet of paper.

How dare you try to tell me how to be, Mum, when you weren't really there?

Are you seriously asking me for a favour, Joe, after you left me out in the cold until Dad came home? The answer is NO!

Can you please not speak to me like that? Please? It makes me anxious, and there's no need.

I can help you with your homework on Saturday, right now I need some time for myself.

The list went on and on with frustrated attempts at standing his ground. Jacob remembered how stepped on, disregarded, and taken advantage of he'd felt. He didn't know how to get himself out of his conundrum. Just as had happened in rooms one and two, he discovered things about himself, his journey, and potentially his future. In this one, it was no different. Bill had mentioned this pattern to him many times, but something didn't quite seem to click. *"All part of the therapeutic journey,"* Bill had said to me. *It made sense, but I became angry with him too. I wanted to tell him a few phrases from this letter, but as usual, I lacked the courage to do so.*

Jacob was deep in thought and hadn't noticed the pieces of paper falling on the floor around him. He snapped out of his emotionally-charged daydream. *More like a day-night-mare,* he thought. He picked up the paper and grabbed a pen from the desk opposite the chair he was sitting on.

He suddenly understood the purpose of this third room— those things that remained unsaid. Those things still hurt him deeply. He needed to get rid of them, to free himself from their trapping forces. He deeply felt the unforgiveness and the pain and ruminated about what would've happened if he was more outspoken and if he'd stood his ground.

He felt the need to speak up, something he'd never done. As Bill said about everything, "That would take practice." That concept would take a lot of getting used to and a lot of courage he felt he didn't have yet. But how would he build on it without testing it out first?

A new chair became obvious to Jacob opposite to where he was sitting. It hadn't been there before. He'd learned in the past few days not to be shocked by much in that place— from his stuff being there to the way the intruders manifested in the first room—*An utterly bizarre experience, if you ask me. How would I ever describe that to anyone?*—to a peculiar but fascinating flower and series of comic strips in the second room, to magically appearing pieces of paper and chairs. Why on earth would anything surprise him anymore?

Jacob noticed some pieces of paper sitting on that chair with a pen lying on top. *Ah, the classic empty chair.* Bill had explained it to him, but he had been averse to trying it. *How embarrassing and odd to suggest such a thing*, he'd thought a few months ago when Bill suggested it to him at the end of a session. They'd been discussing breaches of his boundaries—of course, Jacob had said something more colourful, but Bill had reframed it like that. Jacob had cursed much more freely in many of his more recent sessions, finding his hours with Bill very reassuring and safe enough to do so. The first time he'd done that, Jacob blushed so much he felt he was burning up. Bill had been sympathetic enough to turn away and fetch him some water. He took long enough to allow Jacob to recover, which was appreciated. That made Jacob feel empowered to curse as he pleased. He was paying a hefty amount for his sessions, after all.

Ok. I'm here on my own. I will do this. Again, as with the other rooms, I don't think there's any other way but through this odd experience. He got up to confirm his suspicions; the door was locked with no key in sight. *I'm the key,* he thought. It was like those escape room experiences his friend was always trying to lure him into. He had kindly declined, as it meant speaking up, talking to other people, daring to venture a guess—out loud—to others who might find them silly, even though some of the escape room scenarios he'd heard about were absolutely silly themselves.

He was stalling, and he knew it.

Jacob got up and paced around a few times. Realising it was getting darker and darker outside, he decided to just get on with it. He might be rewarded with a decent night's sleep. He might need it if he woke up here again without any more rooms to work through or any clear guidance anywhere of what was next. *That would be horrifying,* he thought. *Enough of that today, another Scarlett O'Hara moment needed—"I'll think about that tomorrow,"* she'd say.

Jacob began writing his first note to his brother, who'd always demeaned and bullied him when their father wasn't watching:

Hi, bro. Just wanted to tell you I forgive you. But before I do that, I need to tell you how much you hurt me. There are so many things that you could've done when we were growing up to make it easier for me, things you could've kept to yourself. I realise now you were angry and there were things that you couldn't help. After all, you are older, and you saw more of what happened to Mum. I never knew any different. All those years ago, what I really wanted to say to you was:

"Stop this. Why don't you acknowledge your own issues instead of taking them out on me?"

"You're so mean. Nobody is ever going to want to be your friend."

"If you ever talk to me like that, I am not going to speak to you ever again. In fact, let's try it right now. I'll not speak to you for a week unless you start being nicer to me right now."

Jacob carried on writing more sincere commentary like that, things he wanted to say but couldn't out of fear of retribution, of things getting worse, or of losing his brother. He was lonely as it was; bullying from him was better than nothing. As he worked on the sheet, he used more colourful language, getting his anger out on the paper—he even made a hole in one part of it when he released what had been in there for so long.

Once he'd finished that letter, he moved to the other chair, as Bill had mentioned he would do if they actually carried out the exercise. This exercise was much harder to do, especially on his own, without any reassuring words from Bill or anyone else. *Guess I'll have to encourage myself. Alone yet again. Except for my imaginary brother sitting there, writing to me. This is what I'd like him to say:*

Dear Jacob, I am really sorry I made you feel that way.

I really didn't mean to. I thought we both understood each other because we had the same parents. I guess not.

I might have envied you for having missed the worst bits of Mum's ordeal. And that envy turned into me taking my anger out on you.

I realise now, from reading your deep, heartfelt words of anger, resentment, sadness, that I wasn't good to you at all.

I could've been a better brother to you. Having to deal with Mum not being completely there, and when she was, she'd only talk to you about her churchy things.

I'm glad Dad was there for you; he protected you from me, the big, bad bully. It still doesn't justify things, though, and for that, I'm really regretful.

As Jacob wrote the words and read them out loud as if it was his brother speaking, he felt upset but also relieved. The upset was that he'd never heard—and never expected to hear—those words from his brother, ever. The relief was because he got what he needed out of the exercise: a way to release his anger, sadness, and resentment towards his brother and all that it had done to him through the years. He resented the friendships he didn't get out of fear of being bullied down the line. He resented he didn't have his brother to talk to, to rely on, like he knew some of his friends did. There was so much that could've gone different but didn't.

Enough! he thought, wiping tears from his eyes. He hated crying. He couldn't help it, though, so he gave up on trying. Instead, he curled up in a ball on the floor while a puddle of his tears formed on one of the flowers on the carpet.

After what felt like an eternity, Jacob slowly picked himself up—he'd been prone to making himself light-headed in the past. As he got up, he felt like he was leaving a heavy load of emotional baggage on the floor, and with it, felt lighter. Exhausted from crying and a bit cold—a reaction to crying, as his body recalibrated after releasing what had been held so tight for long enough—Jacob gathered the other papers and thought he would work on those once he returned home. He knew he could do it. He didn't feel as ashamed of his tears anymore, although he might need Bill to get him lots of glasses of water, or at least turn away, while he worked through some of those things.

Jacob was pleased with his progress in that room. It was still hard to get his head around everything that had happened during his few days there—which felt like months— but he'd learned to just sit with it, do whatever was hinted at to him. He'd say he did whatever was asked of him, but that would be lying; he figured it all out on his own. *And that was worthy of noting*, he thought with a smile on his face.

Even so, there's a lot of work to be done, Jacob thought as he left the room to lie down for what he hoped was the last time in that bed, in that house, with those rooms.

A NEW LIFE

The ordeal of the few days in the strange house had left the three exhausted but somewhat renewed as well.

None of them had known they'd wake up in that place. While they were all in separate places, they had similar experiences. They didn't know what being in those places would mean a new life.

Would they be changed forever once they woke up? Would they wake up back in their own homes, or was there something left for them to do?

As the night ended, the birds started singing, the flowers opened up, and the light seeped into their rooms. They got up, expecting to be in their own beds, but realised very quickly they were still in the vicinity of the beckoning rooms.

They weren't finished yet. There was one more thing they needed to do.

CHAPTER 13

Jenna

Jenna woke up in the same way she'd done on the first night but aware the way out of the bed wasn't the left side but the right. She learned that with a big bruise on her forehead that made her aware of where she was. *Definitely not at home*, she thought as she got up for what would turn out to be the last time in that weirdly magical house.

She got dressed, and as she opened the door to the room, she noticed the doors weren't there anymore. It was like she was walking into a different environment altogether. *What the hey? How can this be? The rooms were right there. I went in there, didn't I?* Jenna started to doubt herself like she'd done many times before. This time, though, she remembered that she wasn't powerless, that she could trust herself to work it out, as she had done with the contents of each of the three rooms she'd encountered.

Sounds were coming from the front door. *It's wide open! I can hear the outside now! Not sure what the outside will bring, but it means I'm free. Hang on . . . was I ever really trapped in here? Was this always the plan? I've never heard of anyone having something like this happen—well, except Ebenezer Scrooge, of course, but he had the three ghosts. I didn't have anyone at all in here with me. Besides, that was fiction, right? Or was it? I don't know. I just know I'm not a fictional character, and what happened here the last few days was very real and very odd.* Jenna had been walking while those thoughts ran through her mind. She'd grabbed her music box before she made her way toward the front door.

It was very bright through the front door. Jenna opened it fully, feeling its full weight as she did. The light from outside was unlike anything she'd ever seen before. It was actually all she could see. Taking a deep breath, Jenna took a step forward and walked into her new life.

• • •

Jenna found herself walking down her parents' road. Unsure of what she'd do when she reached their house, she reminded herself of all she'd gained from the beckoning rooms. While still holding onto the music box, she thought, *Boy, will they be shocked when they see this! They took it away from me along with everything else, but here I am, holding it as if it was brand new. The "me" pre-rooms would've wanted to give them an earful, to tell them how much it hurt, but as I know, it doesn't bode well for me to do that. It will always be counterproductive because the gaslighting gets stronger and stronger the more I try to state my case. Best to leave it alone. I'm not sure why I've come out of the, uhm—the beckoning house?—to this situation right here. What do I need to do here with these two? Let's see what happens.*

Jenna was two houses away from her parents' home when she heard her mother: "Jenna? Is that you? What are you doing here? We weren't expecting you. The house is a mess. You should've let us know you were coming."

And there it is. I did something wrong. Already. That was quick.

Jenna saw her mum glance over at the music box in her hands, with a puzzled look on her face, and went a little pale. Her mum seemed to lack understanding or words, so she just stared and pointed towards it.

"What's the matter, Mum? Looks like you've seen a ghost. Oh, I see. You've noticed my music box. I found it in this house I was just in for the last few days. I'd tell you more about it, but you wouldn't believe me. You'd say that I've been reading my fantasy books again and that I should grow up."

"When have I ever said that to you?" Mum started.

"You used to say that to me all the time, Mum, but it doesn't matter. I've made my peace with it. I just came along to let you know, uhm, to, let you know ... that I won't be coming over that often. It feels better for me to stay away for a while. I know it might not work for you, but it's time I started thinking about myself."

Her mum was speechless while she listened to Jenna and heard music coming from the music box. It was almost like the Valkyrie song. A war song, but a war without bloodshed—one in which there was finally peace.

Jenna approached her mum tentatively; she didn't know what would happen if she got any closer. Sometimes she'd get pushed away or shouted at. It really depended on her mum's mood that day and maybe even how she felt about Jenna's "childish ways." This time, though, it was different. With her mum in shock, Jenna managed to give her a hug. She squeezed as hard as she could, knowing that it would be one of the last times she'd see her. It needed to be done. She knew her mum would never change, but now she had more control over what to do about it. *Distance might actually make the heart grow fonder*, she thought as she released her hug on her mum and turned around to wave at her dad, who was watching, glued to the spot on the front porch. She blew him a kiss, and as she started walking back the way she'd come, she was smiling the biggest smile she'd ever had, the only one after an encounter with her mother.

Jenna found her way back home after a train and a few bus changes. She found her keys—miraculously in her pocket. *What else would I expect after the days I've just had?* She smiled as she unlocked her front door, cherishing the memory of those three strange friends she'd made while finding herself in the myriad of difficult memories, thoughts, and emotions. She knew she'd never be the same again.

She was ready to live her new life in full.

CHAPTER 14

Jeremiah

Sitting on the top bunk bed, the same one he'd fallen off just a few days ago, Jeremiah thought about his options. He still wasn't in his bed. He didn't know if he was trapped or not. Jeremiah wasn't sure whether he wanted to find out just yet. It was a catch 22. *I hate catch 22s. Nobody wins. And in this case, I don't win, and I really despise losing. What do I do?!*

After a while of trying to jump out of bed but being unable to, he decided to use the ladder on the side for once. Jeremiah figured it would probably buy him some time, allow him to think about what to do.

It didn't work. Jeremiah reached the bottom of the stairs and still had no solution to his current predicament. *Now, the only choice is to open this door like I did four days ago and face whatever is there.* He was already standing in front of the bedroom door when he finished this thought.

Before opening the door, Jeremiah grabbed the journal that had been his friend for so long in the past and had helped him understand his purpose during his time in the house. He opened the door and felt the warmth of the light coming from the outside, in the direction of the front door. "The front door is wide open!" he shouted with excitement. "Am I free to go?" he asked in the empty house. No reply; only a few birds could be heard on the outside.

Without taking any chances, Jeremiah ran towards the front door, stopping for only a second, quickly studying the bright light that was the only thing he could see. Jeremiah decided he would take his chances and ran into the bright light.

• • •

Crossing the threshold was the easy part. Landing in the middle of an AA meeting was certainly not. *Oh, crap! Seriously? I get out of that house and land straight here? Couldn't I have had some time to think about it? I guess not. Aw well, now is as good a time as any.*

Jeremiah sat in the back row, trying to go unnoticed. He failed miserably; it seemed everyone knew one another there. Anyone new would be sticking out like a sore thumb. And in this case, he was the sore thumb. Flashing his best nervous smile, he waved at the people waving back at him from the snacks table. They motioned him over, pointing at a hot drink, offering him one.

He got up, shook their hands, and introduced himself. He was shaking, but the ease at which these people were relating to him made him feel calmer as each moment passed. They asked him why he was there. Jeremiah said, "Well, I wasn't planning on coming here, but something almost literally threw me in here." He didn't quite know how to explain his experience for the last few days. That would have to do. They wouldn't believe him anyway. *Would they?*

"Ah, yes. I've had that same feeling before. The first time I ended up in one of these meetings, I felt like a zombie, stumbling along, looking for the next drink. Instead, I managed to crawl into a meeting and get myself sobered up. Of course, I'm making it sound simpler than it actually is. But seriously, it's great you're here. Acknowledging that you've got a problem is the first and most crucial step. Well done, mate!"

Jeremiah smiled at the man and excused himself. It was too much for him, but he also felt like it was the right time. *It is the right time*, he repeated to himself, under his breath. Lost in thought, he hadn't noticed the meeting had begun. The man he'd been talking to came over to him, gently placed his hand on his shoulder, and helped him to his seat. He respected the spot Jeremiah had chosen earlier—at the very back, safe from being stared at from behind or called up to speak straight away.

Jeremiah knew how these things went. People would get up to talk about their journey, how they were doing, how they were keeping sober, or if they'd relapsed, have a few tears, and got support from the group. He felt like he had in the house and so many times in the past—wanting to curl up on the floor and rock himself to sleep or go into a daze, which meant he was there but also really wasn't. He knew this wasn't a possibility when he heard the meeting master say, "I see we have a newcomer. I wonder if you'd mind introducing yourself to the group."

He knew he couldn't get out of it. Jeremiah stood up slowly, considering whether to make a run for the door. *Don't be silly*, he said to himself. *These people won't hurt you. Just go for it. Pretend you're writing in your journal or something.* Jeremiah got to the front and spoke words he never thought he'd say; he even shed a few tears as he opened up to the room full of strangers, telling them things he'd never said out loud before.

"When I was younger, it was really tough for me." Others nodded in acknowledgment of how hard it had been for them as well. This reassured Jeremiah that he wasn't alone, so he continued. "I was told everything I did was wrong, and so I ended up doing the thing that was the most wrong of all—drinking. I had awful anger issues that I now understand were justified. It was hard with my mother; she wasn't very understanding, and then my grandmother died, and that meant I was even more on my own, with no one to get what was happening to me." Without wanting to say too much about the last few days, he spoke about his journaling and how that had helped him. "This journal I'm holding, I thought I'd lost it forever. But something happened in the last few days that reacquainted me with it. It's been quite a whirlwind of a few days; you wouldn't believe it if I told you. That's how I found you guys today. I kinda fell in here, if you see what I mean. Anyway, I guess I have to say it now, right?" Everyone nodded, hopeful for him to start his journey into sobriety.

"I am Jeremiah, and I'm an alcoholic."

CHAPTER 15

Jacob

Oh, no! Jacob thought as he woke up. *Still here. Still not at home.* He wanted to cry, to scream, to go back to his old scaredy-cat habits, but something inside of him was different. He was able to keep breathing and keep at least a little bit of rationality while struggling with his realisation that he wasn't safe at home yet. *Breathe in for four, hold for two, out for four. Rinse and repeat.* He kept saying to himself as he paced around the now-familiar bedroom.

Jacob looked out the window. The garden was still there, more beautiful than ever. A door was flapping in the wind. *Can I go out there?* He made his way downstairs, sliding down the banister like he had wanted to do before, and ran out the back of the house, not realising that the front door was also open.

The garden was incredible. Jacob could only wish to create something like this himself. He spent a long time out there, looking at the flowers, smelling them, admiring their shapes, colours . . . *Their majestic calm,* he thought.

Eventually, he wandered back into the house and saw the front door open. Bright light the only thing he could see from where he was standing. Hesitantly, he moved slowly closer, inching his way over, taking careful step after careful step. Confidence would take a while to build. *But at least I'm not frozen anymore. Progress!*

Holding on to the flowers he'd picked from the garden, he put his hand in front of him—like you would if you were walking in a dark room, feeling for what is in front of you, keeping safe from bumping into danger. He crossed the threshold of the big door and found himself in the waiting room. *Bill's waiting room. Oh, thank God! I need a debrief after the past few days. But will he believe me? How will I even begin?*

Jacob sat down and waited for his session time. He kept going over and over in his head about how he would tell Bill about what had happened. *There's no way he'll believe me. This is insane! Should I just leave? Nah, I need to talk. I've spent four days speaking to myself. A bit of reality and human connection is absolutely necessary.*

Bill came out and called him in. They shook hands as they'd agreed to do from the first session. Quietly made their way into the room. Well, briefly quiet as Jacob began speaking even before the door was shut behind him for the first time ever.

"Ok," Bill said. These were always his first few words. They'd agreed on this, as well. Jacob had needed a lot of "scaffolding," as a teacher would call it. He needed a lot of hand-holding while he learned to feel safe in the therapy room and with the therapist himself. They'd spent a lot of time playing Mastermind while Jacob found his voice and could start to piece together a few sentences, describing what he was experiencing and how things were for him.

Bill started, of course, with the safest and most familiar thing he knew; the zombies game. That's what Bill called it. He could never remember the name of the game. Jacob was glad he at least remembered some of it. Nobody else seemed to care about his special interest in zombies. *Maybe that's what I should start with today,* he thought. So he did.

"You remember, when I started talking to you, I'd spend most of our session talking about the zombie apocalypse game, right?"

"Right," Bill said.

"Ok, so I had some experience of that the last few days. Like, literally!" Jacob always spoke like he was a few years younger than he was when he was with Bill. Maybe he was "regressing" when he was in sessions. *Who cares? It works, right?* Jacob carried on, explaining what had happened.

Bill sensitively took it all in, leaning forward, paying close attention. He asked questions about the fantastical stories Jacob shared, never judging, never showing how freaked out he probably was about what he was hearing.

Jacob asked for some paper and crayons. Bill obliged. As the session continued, Jacob began to draw what he'd experienced. From the thunder and lightning to the talking flowers to the glowing yellow flower that turned beige to the comic strips and the flowery empty chair exercise he'd been subjected to by who-knows-who. Everything came alive in his drawings.

Jacob could always communicate better with drawings. *Maybe that's why the second room spoke to me in comic strips. Drawings!* He smiled as he was drawing. He told Bill it was because he had just realised how clever his experience had been. From the moment he woke up, with the beautiful garden outside to help him calm down with what he saw, to the way the comics slowly took him from his past to his future— healing had happened in that house. He couldn't explain it. But neither could he explain how he'd moved forward during his sessions with Bill. Maybe he didn't need to put it into words.

It was what it was. There was nothing that needed to be said. It was an experience.

My Journey. My terms. I will move at my pace.

FROM THE AUTHOR

What's in a dream? That's the question that I pose to you today. Don't think of this as a random question, but as one that would trigger your thoughts and lead you to delve into the exploration of the meaning of dreams and how this relates to therapy and, therefore, to the unconscious. More importantly, how dreams and therapy relate to the book you're holding in your hands right now—*The Beckoning Rooms*.

Covering my counselling training have been a blanket of psychoanalytic theories and wonderful tutors who made these theories come alive. I am integrative in practice, but at my core, I will always have an analytical mind when it comes to exploring the unconscious and the issues my clients bring me.

Let me take you back to 2003-2004. I started seeing my very first clients at the university clinic in Guatemala and decided to start my own therapy process. There were personal and professional reasons for this. I won't go into details as that's between my therapist and me.

I had about a year of sessions with this therapist. She was very traditionally psychoanalytic, so she didn't say much to me, which suited me just fine. The things she did say stick in my mind even now and have been a great source of comfort to me ever since. That's the power of therapy. At the end of this batch of therapeutic work, I started talking about a particular topic (again, I won't disclose what it was, sorry) and tried to open up about it, but it was still not time. So I "legged" it out of there to never return.

In 2009, I embarked on another counselling course so I could work in the United Kingdom as a therapist. I believe now, looking back, my counselling training in Guatemala would have been enough to start, but I needed to find my way around the UK way of life and working. Taking on this course meant another batch of therapy, this time for the duration of the course, as a requirement to graduate. That was fine by me as there were things I needed to work on.

There always is something to work on as the unconscious material from our past beckons us. Sometimes gently. Sometimes more forcefully. There came a point when the aforementioned "particular topic" came up again, and it was hard. I believe my words to my therapist were, "I really don't want to go there, but here we are, we might as well do it." She checked with me (this one also didn't say much, but what she said is still having an impact to this day): "Are you sure you want to talk about that?"

I said yes, probably a crying blubbering mess at that point. What happened during the next few weeks of opening the proverbial Pandora's box was quite something!

I used to have a recurring dream where I'd always appear in a house. The house was familiar to me. I wasn't in a strange place or anything—I knew the place. It was either my house or a friend's house. Lurking somewhere in the building, there was always a room, a door that I was wary of.

What made me wary of it was a mystery to me. In the years I had the dream, I couldn't figure it out! I could never go into that room or even go near it. It gave me the creeps. I felt really anxious and had a sense of dread about what I might find if I opened that door. I'm unsure of what else happened in those recurring dreams. It felt like I was in the house for a long time—maybe a typical day, with normal things going on.

It's been a while since I've had that dream. I know what stopped it was talking about "that topic" in therapy, hence, as I mentioned before, the power of therapy! I've not dreamt that dream ever since those hard sessions, where everything in life felt surreal for a few weeks, but something released.

That unconscious part of myself had lost its power. It had lost its ability to haunt me in my waking and sleeping hours. I know that there are many more things to explore about "the topic" as there always will be—the unconscious is vast and will strike whenever and however it wants. This is why I find therapy so precious—as a process I've gone through myself— and as a process I support for my counselling clients.

In the story I've just told you, talking through something in therapy made a recurring dream stop. The symbolism in dreams is truly incredible. I've seen it in my own dreams and life and in my clients' dreams and lives. What we dream says something about who we are, what we've sent to the repressed bin of our minds, and what we must deal with before it deals with us.

The end of my recurring dream after that batch of therapy led me to write *The Beckoning Rooms*. The idea first came to me a few months after that therapy process.

ACKNOWLEDGEMENTS

I would like to thank my husband, Shaun, for his patience and support throughout all our time together. He's amazing, and I couldn't have done it without him.

To all the people that have been here for the ride—friends, family, colleagues, tutors. You all have played a big part in my journey, which has led me to become an author of two books so far, with a few more in the inkpot.

To the Igniting Souls London and UK crowd in particular, but to the whole Igniting Souls Tribe, for being inspirational individuals with a variety of talents, skills, and encouragement they're not shy to share.

To my beta readers and to those that wrote the endorsements and reviews you see at the front of this book. Thank you for your honesty and dedication in this journey.

This novel wouldn't have been possible without the grace of God, so I'd like to thank Jesus for allowing me to reach all of you in this way.

ABOUT THE AUTHOR

Karin Brauner is passionate about helping people get on track—or back on track—in their personal and professional lives through practical tools and inspirational conversations in a variety of settings.

Karin teaches tools that she's learned and developed throughout her life. She knows how hard things can get and how great things can be once you move through to the other side.

She now shares the knowledge she's gained through various mediums to show people a path to better self-care, support when processing their past, and working out their present so they can lead an improved life and thrive in their personal and professional relationships.

Connect at karinbrauneronline.co.uk/beckoningrooms

The Beckoning Rooms Experience

You've read the book, now it's your turn.

You're in.
The only way out is to solve
the puzzles.

Join Jenna, Jeremiah and Jacob
as they explore their beckoning
rooms, in the hope of getting
back home.

The past beckons.
Will you take up the
challenge?

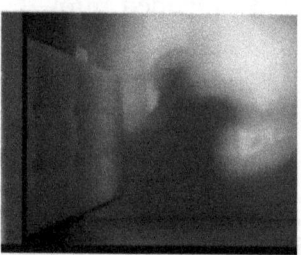

Play the game at
beckoningroomsexperience.karinbrauneronline.co.uk/
wp/welcome/

Dreaming Up the Repressed

A Beckoning Rooms Prequel

They were wide awake when they encountered the beckoning rooms, but as they slept their dreams also beckoned.

Download the complete prequel at karinbrauneronline.co.uk/prequel/

What's in a Dream
Blog Post Series

Ever since I was a child, I had dreamt a recurring dream. In this dream, there was always a house. In each dream, in each house, there was a room that made me wonder what was behind there that was so mysterious. It beckoned me to find out, but something kept me from finding the answer.

After a batch of therapy years later, and touching on a topic I couldn't speak of in my previous therapy process, the dreams stopped.

That's where The Beckoning Rooms comes in. This book is a consequence of my own personal journey, but also of my counselling career, seeing the effects of working through dreams and the past with my clients.

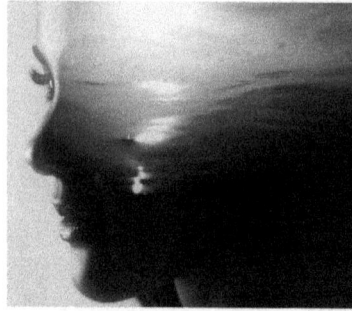

This blog post series will lead you deeper into the world of dreams, and how you can find the meaning behind them. It also gives insights into psychoanalytic theory and how it looks in practice.

Read the whole series at
karinbrauneronline.co.uk/dreamblogs/

Mini-Courses

Did the topics touched upon in the novel leave you wanting to find out more about how to deal with them and other topics?

I've created mini-courses with lots of information, reflection points, print-outs, check-lists, and more.

Creating and Living a more Compassionate Life

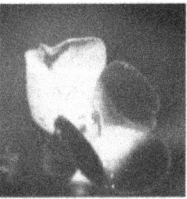

Anger: Fear it or befriend it

Find Your Own Way To Grieve

Self-Esteem and Neurodiversity

What you need to know to help your child thrive in a mainstream world

karinbrauneronline.co.uk/mini-courses

20 Self-Care Habits

Develop your Strengths, Use your Resources, Improve your life and Relationships

Self care is important.

Not just the usual having a bath or having a nice cup of your favourite tea.

I mean the real stuff.

The stuff that makes your life fulfilling and happy, or the stuff that makes you have the opposite experience.

In this book I give you 20 in-depth ways in which you can develop self-care habits that will improve your life and your relationships.

There are strengths in all of us that might have been quietened down or simply not put to any use due to life circumstances – being told you have to say yes all the time; or people denying your needs and/or feelings, which led to you not expressing either.

Reflecting on these 20 habits, and putting them into practice, in your own time, will allow you to learn more about yourself and how you relate with others.

karinbrauneronline.co.uk/20habits/

Self-Care Coaching

Delve deeper into your self-care journey...
The book has changed lives.
The Programmes will take you even further

Disclaimer: There is no quick fix!
A mindset change will take a bit of
time but it's not impossible.

This mindset re-set will
change your whole life. Trust
me, I've seen it in my own
life, and in the lives of my
clients!

Why should we fit in a box
someone else made
somewhere in the ether?

Truth is – we don't!

By working on our boundaries and learning how to meet our
needs, we get to know who we really are and how we want to
live our lives to the fullest.

https://karinbrauneronline.co.uk/self-care/

Thank you for reading The Beckoning Rooms and checking out the bonus content.

I trust it will be entertaining, informative and helpful in your own journey.

My aim with writing the novel was to bring awareness about our unconscious world and how it might affect us even years later. Even when we've forgotten the things that lie beneath our consciousness.

Has The Beckoning Rooms left you wondering about your own past and how to safely explore it?

There are many ways to do so:

- Reading books on a particular topic you might need to learn more about
- Find online courses that will help you on your journey
- Finding a counsellor
- Talking to friends and family you trust
- Journaling
- and more...

Engaging in counselling is about much more than dealing with a crisis. Through counselling you can find out more about yourself - who you are, what you want and need from life and relationships, and so much more. You are the guide in this journey, a counsellor is there to support you through what you might discover.

Email and Text Based Counselling
k-brauner-counselling.co.uk